YUICHI SIN

DON'T GIVE INTO FEAR

Don't Give Into Fear
Hollywood Horror, Movie Stars, Machetes, and Satanic Rituals.

©2021 Yuichi Sin

print ISBN: 978-1-09836-452-6
ebook ISBN: 978-1-09836-453-3

CONTENTS

CHAPTER 1	1
CHAPTER 2	5
CHAPTER 3	8
CHAPTER 4	20
CHAPTER 5	24
CHAPTER 6	28
CHAPTER 7	32
CHAPTER 8	34
CHAPTER 9	37
CHAPTER 10	45
CHAPTER 11	53
CHAPTER 12	60
CHAPTER 13	68
CHAPTER 14	74
CHAPTER 15	77
CHAPTER 16	81
CHAPTER 17	86
CHAPTER 18	97
CHAPTER 19	104
CHAPTER 20	108
CHAPTER 21	112
CHAPTER 22	115
CHAPTER 23	117
CHAPTER 24	120
CHAPTER 25	132
CHAPTER 26	134

CHAPTER 27	138
CHAPTER 28	148
CHAPTER 29	154
CHAPTER 30	156
CHAPTER 31	159
CHAPTER 32	160
CHAPTER 33	163
CHAPTER 34	167
CHAPTER 35	173
CHAPTER 36	175
CHAPTER 37	177
CHAPTER 38	180
CHAPTER 39	184
CHAPTER 40	189
CHAPTER 41	192
CHAPTER 42	201
CHAPTER 43	203
CHAPTER 44	208
CHAPTER 45	217
CHAPTER 46	221
CHAPTER 47	224
CHAPTER 48	227

CHAPTER 1

S-A-Y. That's my creed. Stay Ahead of Yourself. I didn't invent this—General Patton did.

"Keep marching forward and let the supply lines catch up to you!" he proclaimed. "Whatever you do, don't wait for them!"

Francis Ford Coppola learned it researching *Patton* (1970), and he stuck to it when he ran Zoetrope Studios. Just because the supply lines never caught up to him in that case and the studio starved and died like a resident of District 12 in *The Hunger Games* (2012), it's no reason to discount the concept.

I passed by the old studio lot—Zoetrope that is, south of Santa Monica Boulevard, Romaine below, Seward on the East and Las Palmas to the West. Google it. Built in 1919, it started life as Hollywood Studios. Coppola shot *One From the Heart* (1981) there, a delightful little confection, so sweet it could make you throw up (needed more blood, like *Apocalypse Now* (1979).

Before Coppola was born, Chaplin, Pickford, Fairbanks and D.W. Griffith all worked there. So did Harold Lloyd and Howard Hughes, and later on Cagney, Cary Grant, Fred Astaire, Laurel and Hardy, Mae West, but you don't care about that—nobody does. Old hat, dead people, Hollywood ghosts. History is for losers, right? *I Love Lucy* was filmed there, then the Coppola years (like *two* years). A bunch of TV garbage followed: *Jeopardy, Pee-wee's Playhouse* (actually, I liked that show), *Star Search*. George Burns had an office in one of the bungalows from 1920 till the day he died—showed up for work every day, too. It's been Hollywood Studios, Metropolitan

Studios, Zoetrope Studios, Hollywood Center Studios, and now it's Sunset Las Palmas Studios—they gave up on fancy names and finally just went with "easy-to-find-location-name."

That's right—*people* make movies; they don't "just appear." It's a manufacturing process like making refrigerators, though not as organized and not in China (as much).

They still shoot things at the studio.

Yeah, okay, you caught me—on the one hand I'm all about S-A-Y, Stay Ahead of Yourself, which sounds like forward thinking if anything does—on the other hand I'm obsessed with old, arcane Hollywood stuff—well that's me, a puzzle all over. All over the map. Google me—I'm on every page. Enigma wrapped in a question mark.

My name is Jack C. Cunningham. I know, it sounds like a phony name—because it *is* a phony name. I made it up; I can't use my real name, and not because I'm wanted by the FBI or anything (the fools!). I had to make up a phony name on account of my real name was taken by somebody else who joined the Actors Guild before I did (I just got in, thank you very much!), so he gets his real name and I get this. The "C" is to differentiate me from all the other Jack Cunningham actors out there—all nobodies; I'm not worried. I'm twenty-five years old and that's all I will tell you right now, except to say I'm devastatingly handsome, and it's not just me saying that. Ever since I was a child people have commented on my good looks, saying "you should be in the movies."

So that's what I'm doing!

Somewhere on Willoughby I hurried to catch up with one of my acting buddies, Clyde Something-or-Other. We study with Freddy Weaver, one of the best acting coaches in Hollywood—you've probably heard of him. Not that I really need an acting coach. I'm a natural. Naturally talented. Everybody says so. "Handsome and talented." But acting classes are the way to network, find out about roles, get to know all the other up-and-coming talents—you know, *hustle*. That's the name of the game in this town in case you didn't know already—*hustle*.

I know what it takes to be a "player" in Hollywood, and the only reason I'm not there yet is because of a lot of baggage and some particular bastards holding me back.

"How's it going, Clyde?" I asked my pal.

"Okay," he answered noncommittally, and walked a little faster, like maybe he didn't want to talk to me right then, which I pegged right away meant he was keeping some sort of secret.

"Any auditions?" I asked, taking a stab.

"Well, yeah," he said with a sigh, slowing. Busted. "I had an audition for a sit-com last week and an audition for a cable drama lined up next week. Not sure which one I want if I get them both."

I said nothing. The chance of Clyde What's-His-Name getting an actual paying acting gig was about as likely as me having to work at Ralph's, which, by-the-way, is where Clyde can be found stocking fruits and vegetables in the produce section every weekday morning from 7:30 to 11:00 at the store on Vermont. I knew about that, too.

"How about you?" Clyde asked, just to be polite.

Even though we were the best of friends, I knew he didn't give a rat's ass about me. It's every man for himself, lemme tell ya.

"My agent wants me to do a film in Italy," I told him. "It's the lead and it's a good role—'sunbaked love story' or something like that. The script is genius. The whole thing'd be Oscar-bait if it were American, but Italian? I don't know. And right in the middle of pilot season."

"I hear you," Clyde said, walking a little faster again, my success instantly signaling his pea-brain to shift into a higher gear if he b to be anything but a pathetic loser in this world.

"I'd probably still audition if the part was good," I went on, "but mostly I wait for my reputation to proceed me. Since I started working as

3

a manager—which is where the real money is—I don't have much time for acting anyway."

I let him go on ahead. I wasn't going to waste energy on a sprint with Clyde Nobody.

So yeah, that's right, I'm a manager now. So far just one client, but she's a handful, no pun intended—she's actually on the skinny side and no, I haven't touched her.

Her name is Rayna Rourke, which isn't her real name, of course, and she was there early at acting class as usual, doing her warm-up exercises: neck roll, shoulder roll, chest expansion, waist twist, bends, breathing, vocalizing, the whole nine yards. It was all a waste of time as far as I was concerned. Freddy had a dozen warm-up games and improvs and you-name-it to take up the first half of the acting class, so warming up before the warm-up was a joke anyway.

"Hey, Rayna," I called to her and she nodded to me the way she always did, noncommittally, secretly, like a couple of spies behind enemy lines. Anybody watching would guess we were just casual acquaintances and nothing more—she was just that good of an actress!

Of course Rayna was in love with me—both a blessing and a curse. Women just adore me. That's the way it is and there's nothing I can do about it.

CHAPTER 2

Depending on who you ask, Hollywood is all sorts of things. Beyond the "Dream Factory" blather there's an actual city—though not officially (nothing in Hollywood is "official"), with all its own city problems, embedded right inside the larger city of Los Angeles. It's also the people, on the prowl mostly, trying to make it one way or another—actors, musicians, performers, stuntmen, plus behind-the-scenes, behind-the-camera personnel—cameramen, set dressers, script supervisors, sound people, boom operators, accountants, all concerned with getting a film or TV-show shot. And even before that happens, hundreds of producers, bankers, agents, and money-men are involved, then after, there are editors, sound editors, foley artists, titles, distributors, lawyers, ad-men, publicists.

Like everything important in L.A., it started out as real estate, a housing project, a way to make a quick buck. For many, it's still that way, but for most illusions of magic have seeped into the brain like encephalitis, so when they think of Hollywood they think of riches and stardom and love and sex and desire—"The Silver Screen" and all that. Of course, the by-products of actual silver mining—arsenic, lead, cadmium, zinc—all poisonous—can kill you.

The Hollywood of today won't be the same next week. Buildings go down, others go up. But many of the old places are still there, or their names are at least—The Roosevelt Hotel, Grauman's Chinese, Musso and Frank's, Columbia Records. The seediness lingers from the 1920s to today—graft, prostitution, gambling, sexual deviancy of all stripes. Danger lurks around every corner and despite the Chamber of Commerce protestations and LAPD declarations of victory, the heart of Hollywood is not a safe place.

It's likely Rayna Rourke knew some of this when she arrived in town via train. From Union Station she took a city bus down Cesar Chavez turning to Sunset—Downtown to Echo Park to Silverlake to Thai Town and Little Armenia to Hollywood, where she was last seen.

Later, when the records were unsealed, it was discovered that "Rayna Rourke" was in fact born Julie Baker, in Nekoosa, Wisconsin, north of Petenwell Lake. According to the court, her name was never legally changed. Later, when the insatiable press stirred her history into a tornado of morbid curiosity, it was discovered she had downloaded and filled out a state name-change request. She had not, however, made a first appearance with the court clerk to file for the transformation.

"I need something more exotic," she posted to friends on Facebook a month after her arrival. "There are over 300 'Julie Bakers' on imdb, can U believe it?" (An exaggeration—in fact, there were only 9.)

Rayna was a fresh-faced talent, with a young, innocent look. Within a span of four months she was the star of Freddy Weaver's Actors Studio. Everyone knew she was going places; her talent was said to be "breathtaking."

According to eye-witnesses, on January 13, at the start of pilot season, after class at Freddy's studio, Jack C. Cunningham asked her to coffee at one of the many coffee shops in the area around Santa Monica and La Brea. Rayna accepted—it's not clear why. Maybe it was because Jack was easily the handsomest man in their acting class, which was saying a lot, since Freddy Weaver was known to attract a host of good-looking young men to his classes.

Sometime that same week, according to her roommate at the time, who prefers not to be named, "Rayna asked me if I thought Jack was gay."

"I told her I didn't think so but I'd like to find out," the roommate said. "I said it as kind of a joke, but really, the guy was so handsome, you wouldn't believe it! I don't think he was gay, in fact, more like 'not sexual' if you know what I mean, or 'too busy,' you know? That kind of thing. Some guys are just like that. Low testosterone or something. I told Rayna to fuck him and report back to me."

CHAPTER 3

If you knew my background, you'd be totally amazed at how successful I've made myself. The secret? POSITIVITY! My positivity will see me through as it always has.

My first memory is of being dumped at an orphanage. Night. Dark. Early evening but still pitch black, winter when it gets dark so early. It was a brick building, municipal in style. It could have just as easily been a library or a police station. Six kids to a room. Bunks. Hell. I lived there till I was about five, if you can call that living.

My second memory is being abandoned at the Skully compound, a Satanic nightmare of a place populated by savages of all kinds. Rain. Daytime. A sweltering summer. The smell of wet hay and horseshit.

Mr. Skully was a truck driver, nicknamed "Mack" (ha ha), prone to drink, gone for long periods of time. Mrs. Skully's choice of drugs was amphetamines, then downers, then uppers again, an endless cycle. They abused all of us kids terribly with nightly beatings, starvation, sleep deprivation, you name it. We were chained to the beds, confined to quarters, forced to eat all sorts of ghastly food and drink our own urine.

By design, the Skullys situated their hell-hole out in the middle of nowhere, rural Oregon. That way no one would bother them. There were no neighbors to hear our desperate screams for help. Fortunately for us, and for my own future, mother Skully ("Rose") would often go on one of her benders, and not wanting us around, would let us kids (between two and five of us—it varied) off at the local mall, where it was our responsibility to entertain ourselves. Without money, we soon learned to sneak into the Cinema Multiplex, which is where I caught the "movie bug." As an alternative home and complete universe, the movies served to provide everything my own situation lacked—honesty, emotion, love, beauty, heating and air-conditioning. Sex, too. I learned about sex from the movies, which is the ideal way to learn IMHO.

Infected with a passion for films, I also became entranced with the *history* of film, and the people involved in making them—actors, directors, writers, cinematographers.

The move to Hollywood was inevitable. *Enlisted*, you could say. Joined up with an army of dream-weavers.

Not that anyone here cares about the past. Like this place I'm living, the Arbuckle Hotel—an old apartment building in the heart of Hollywood, an historical landmark as far as I'm concerned, once a fancy hotel. No, it isn't fancy anymore. People say it's haunted, which is true. So many famous people have lived here or checked in for the night to sleep off a drunk or to make whoopee, you can't even count anymore. People also come here to die—still do—mostly overdoses, but a ton of suicides, too. It's only four stories high but you take a swan-dive off the roof, that'll do it for sure—has in every case, AFAIK.

Speaking of the roof, there's an old water-tank up there they've never taken down, which was the last resting place of a certain infamous Mavis Benning, heir to the Virginia Rappe legacy (look her up—what am I—Google?). Mavis was a crack-whore probably, just another actress, whose body took a last soak up there for six months while the residents of the building drank the water and showered in her essence. She was naked, with a frightening array of tattoos, home-made but strangely beautiful, applied post-mortem, according to the coroner. That's right, some sick motherfucker went up there and tattooed dead Mavis in the water tank. For practice.

It wasn't the first murder in the building—the place had a long history, including the notorious unsolved Red Iris Murder which caused such a sensation in the 30s. Serial killers lived there, checking in early in their careers: "The Alley Stabber," "The Zodiac," "Pliers," "The Off-ramp Strangler." They all took a swing at the Arbuckle Hotel before moving on to the big leagues. Only Charlie Manson never seemed to have stayed there, but that may just be from a lack of sufficient research.

Of course, all that was before I moved in—don't blame me for what's not my fault. It was a big scandal when they found Mavis—in all the papers. Of course the apartment management didn't do anything like take the tank down; they just installed a two-dollar padlock which somebody like me with a good cutter could snip apart in a minute.

Lawsuits were filed, people moved out. Nobody could bring themselves to drink the water even though it didn't come from the tank anymore. Snowflakes. That's how I got my deal on my apartment. It's a one-year lease. I figure I'll give it a year and I'll have my own house in the hills by then. And no, I repeat, I had nothing to do with Mavis Banning's death, but thanks for asking.

"May I come in?" Clyde Whoever asked.

"Certainly, Mr. DeWitt..." Rayna answered.

They were doing a scene from *All About Eve* (1950), an odd choice— *Clyde's idea* was my guess. He fancied himself a George Sanders type but he was no George Sanders—too young, too goofy, too skinny ass, totally American, but you had to hand it to him—he was trying to stretch. Rayna had the Anne Baxter part down, at least the innocent ingénue at the start, but could she be the bitch queen at the end? Hard to tell.

"I think the time has come for you to shed some of your humility," Clyde was telling her. He didn't trust her innocence, didn't believe it. Watching, I wasn't so sure either. Would Rayna turn, stab me in the back, bust my balls, turn on me once she got a taste of the good life she was bound to enjoy once the world knew of her talent? Like Eve in the movie? Yeah, she would; who was I kidding?

We went for coffee after class.

"You were really good tonight," I told her, figuring to butter her up a little. Actors need encouragement all the time. They can't get enough of hearing how wonderful they are. It's true of everyone actually, but actors are the worst.

"Thanks," she said shyly, the way she does sometimes, which totally gets me thick and hard.

"You know you were," I answered.

"It's just acting class," she blushed, an affectation I thoroughly appreciate.

"There are no small parts—"

"You're very sweet."

"Cut it out. Let's have a minimum of pretending, okay?"

I'd just quoted *All About Eve* again, and despised the plagiarism. We weren't *All About Eve* (1950), we were *Titanic* (1997). Rayna didn't seem to notice the error. I refocused. E-O-T-P ("Eyes on the Prize"—more on that later).

"So have you been thinking about what we talked about last time?" I asked her. I had the papers with me in a briefcase right down next to my feet, but I didn't take them out right then, afraid of scaring her off. "About me representing you? About me being your manager?"

"I thought about it," Rayna said, and I could see she wasn't convinced yet.

"It's the right thing to do," I told her. "Hesitation is fear. D-G-I-F, remember?"

"Darn-it God, It's Friday?"

I laughed.

"Don't Go In Fear?" she tried again.

"Don't Give Into Fear," I corrected.

Rayna smiled politely. I hated that. I felt like strangling her.

"I'm not comfortable with it, Jack," she said, looking up from her coffee for the first time.

She was afraid of me, I could see that. It was exciting. It also broke my heart.

"Rayna..." I said plaintively, and dared touch her hand, "what's wrong?"

"I talked to an agent today," she said.

I pulled my hand back.

"An agent?"

"Lowanna Xanderson."

I froze. Talk about a knee to the nuts. Lowanna Xanderson was one of the top twenty agents in town, maybe top ten, noted for discovering new talent. The fact that Rayna had even talked to her was a major coup.

"How...?" I stammered.

"You know that play I auditioned for, the Equity waver thing down the street at the Raybill Theatre?"

"That stupid comedy?" I asked. I couldn't believe my ears.

"*Cat's Pause* is the name of it and it isn't stupid. You should have tried out for it—"

"And get stuck in a no-pay play for five weeks of rehearsals and six weeks of begging your friends to come see you—"

"Well, I got a part in the play and it's the lead," Rayna interrupted, getting testy, the way girls do sometimes, "and it turns out the director's a good friend of Lowanna Xanderson's and she invited Lowanna to come watch a rehearsal..."

I kind of tuned out at that point. I could see where this was going. I'd advised Rayna against auditioning for the play—it was just not strategic thinking. She was aiming too low—self-esteem issues, "a little semi-pro dip into desperate theatre at a fire-trap playhouse on Santa Monica Boulevard is all I deserve at this point in my career"—but she'd gone to the audition anyway and it had paid off for her in one of those weird Hollywood happenstance ways and now Rayna was rubbing my face in it like I'd made the mistake of the century and I didn't deserve to be her manager or fuck her nicely for that matter, which was also on my schedule.

"Lowanna thinks I don't really need a manager..." Rayna told me.

I stared. What did I tell you? Already I was in competition with Lowanna *fucking* Xanderson. And don't think the fact was lost on me that Rayna was already calling Lowanna by her first name.

"She told you that?" I asked, a slight squeak in my voice, which I made a note of to avoid from then on.

Rayna nodded. I could tell she wasn't being exactly honest. What Lowanna had no doubt *actually* said was: "Dump this creep. You don't know who he is. *I* don't know who he is. Nobody does. Nobody heard of this guy. Who does he know? What's he gonna do for you?"

I was ready to tear her head off, and Rayna's head, too—

"What she said was..." Rayna began, fortifying herself with coffee. She looked scared again, just by the look on my face. *Good,* I thought—better to be feared than ignored. "She said, 'you're gonna need a manager,' she said, 'and maybe soon, and maybe a PR person and a personal assistant as well, but you're not there yet, and when the time comes I'll get you the top, the best, not...'"

She didn't finish. She gauged my reaction. She'd been about to say "not some unsuccessful, wannabe actor" or "piece of shit" maybe. Okay, I can take a punch, but the fact Rayna was quoting Lowanna Weaver and not speaking for herself didn't make it any less painful or infuriating.

"I like you, Jack," she said sincerely. She swallowed hard, looked away and muttered, "There was no reason for her to call you that."

"Did you tell this agent-person that I'm very successful at what I do, and that I'm very rich?"

"I did. Really."

"And...?"

Rayna fidgeted. She didn't want to answer.

"She was skeptical," Rayna told me in a voice so low I could barely hear her.

I grabbed my briefcase—the one with the management papers in it, the ones I wanted Rayna to sign, which I'd researched on the internet and typed up on my laptop and printed up on my printer—a whole day's work when I could have been doing something else entirely—

"Jack, don't be that way," Rayna called to me as I stormed out of the coffee shop, using all my powers of self-control not to destroy something or someone. With what I had in my pocket at that very moment—

I marched north through the streets of Hollywood, headed nowhere, I thought, but then I was on Fountain, then Sunset, then Franklin, under the 101, past the homeless encampments, up into the hills where my dream-home would be one day if I could just get past the Lowanna Xandersons and Rayna Rourkes and Clyde What's-His-Names and Freddy Weavers of this shit-hole town.

Rayna and I were meant for each other like Vicki Lester and Norman Maine in *A Star is Born* (the original 1937 William Wellman version, not the Gaga one, not to be confused with *What Price Hollywood?* (1932), based on the same story), but unlike those movies, our story would have a happy ending.

But how?

I found my way up a narrow side-street, steep, with ten-million dollar views of the city below. I knew what I had to do, and tonight would be a good night to do it. Cheer me up. The soil under one section of fence had washed away—a mini mudslide; I easily slipped under it and took my position to watch the house, one of those midcentury moderns, all glass, steel and teak-wood, "blurring the line between outdoors and indoors"—you know the real estate pitch.

Not much security, though, not if I could slip so easily in past the fences and the high hedges.

I don't know what the guy did for a living or how he got all the money in the world, but he definitely had it: a ten-million-dollar house, and more importantly to my purposes: a Ferrari in the garage, a 330 GTS, V-12, 300hp, red, excellent to concourse condition I guessed, though I had yet to get close enough to know. Only a hundred of the convertibles were built between 1966 and 1968, according to my research. A half million bucks at retail, the man's pride and joy, which he drove every Sunday morning about noon, never fails, washing it once a month.

I watched the guy for awhile, which settled my heart for the task. I-P-T-B-C, I reminded myself. "It Pays To Be Cautious." Like every evening with this bozo, this night was nothing-burger: he changed into more comfortable clothes from his suit, then made himself dinner. Health food, it looked like, fresh. Watching him from my perch on the hillside just slightly above him, I was beginning to get a little hungry myself. I wished I'd gotten something to eat at the coffee shop instead of wasting my mouth on Rayna.

Despite all his money, the guy looked lonely. If I were that rich, that wouldn't be the way I'd live, alone every night. I'd surround myself with people. There'd be an assistant and a housekeeper and a cook of some kind, and maybe somebody to take care of the grounds full time. They'd be my friends, too, and anytime they wanted to jump in the pool or have a margarita, they'd be welcome as long as they mixed one up for me too. And they'd all be hardbodies so if they wanted to be nude, that would be cool, anytime. In fact, I'd insist on it.

And I wouldn't cook my own food, either. I'd eat out every meal and be rude or ingratiating to the wait staff, depending on my mood and say shit like "and how is the roast duck prepared?"

"Er, 'roasted,'" the waiter would say, dripping with sarcasm, and I'd laugh at him or if it was a her, I'd slap her on the ass hard enough to actually hurt, then tip her some ungodly amount at the end, and then I'd threaten to have her fired so she'd sleep with me sometime down the road—

I waited. Eventually, the rich man shut off the TV and the lights in the front and went back to the back bedroom. He took a book from the nightstand, clicked on the late news and started reading. I waited...patience, remember? Eventually, he went to sleep. I checked the switchblade in my pocket—a necessary evil I hoped wouldn't be necessary—and slipped down the slope, still slightly damp from the last rain. I pulled my jacket up over my face and headed for the front door. I guessed there'd be cameras, but I didn't much care. The key to the house—I'd seen this before—was under the rock on the left side of the farthest ceramic planter. I used it to walk right in. Immediately, I strolled to the alarm and disarmed it using the code I'd observed him use many times previously. With the alarm dead, I pulled the key to the Ferrari off its peg and hurried to the garage. Nary a peep was heard from the back.

The car started right up with a roar and the garage door opened nicely, too. I was down the driveway and through the automatic gate and out onto Sunset in a matter of seconds. If I'd been a car guy or a complete idiot, I might have hit the gas, tried a few turns, checked the handling, pushed it, but I didn't. The top was down; that was thrilling enough for me. As much as I wanted to reproduce a couple of scenes in *Bullitt* (1968), or *The Fast and Furious* franchise (2009-forever), I drove the standard 5MPH over the speed limit, even on the 405—no one noticed.

Jaime's place is in an industrial strip on Parthenia in Northridge (or maybe Reseda—what am I, Google Maps?), San Fernando Valley. It's tucked away amid auto repair shops, lumberyards, storage facilities, plumbing supplies. I pulled up to the massive sliding door at the rear of the property, turned off the engine and immediately felt the cold steel of a pistol pressed into my temple.

"What the hell are you doing?" Jaime wanted to know.

"I brought you a car."

"I didn't order this!"

"It's a Ferrari," I soothed.

"I can see that, moron," he answered.

Jaime Rojo de Luna was a big man with a troubled past, which included prison-time, I suspected, which made him impatient and easy to anger. I was pretty sure he'd killed a few—

"Peace," I told him. "P-E-A-C-E."

"What? Are you drunk?"

"Pause, Exhale, Acknowledge, Choose and Engage. Don't pull the trigger, please. Remember to breathe," I stated as calmly as I could.

"Don't tell me what to do," he barked.

"I wasn't," I said. "I was talking to myself—"

"Get out," he ordered.

I did as I was told.

"I don't want to blast your guts all over this interior..." he stated, signaling me to step away.

I held my hands up as he inspected the vehicle. He was hooked. I could see that.

"Where'd you get this?" Jaime wanted to know.

"From a guy," I answered. "Fresh as a daisy. He won't know it's stolen till he gets up in the morning and maybe not then. Half the time he goes to work without checking on it. You might have till Sunday morning. The pink slip might even be in the glove-box. I never looked."

I could see Jaime liked what I was laying down.

"You're too reckless, dude. I can't have that," Jaime said.

The pistol still hung at his side. I checked my pocket for my blade—assisted opening, quick and easy flip/finger actuated—just in case we had to work this out *Reservoir Dogs* (1992) style. I kept my mitts up a little so he could see I meant no harm, which didn't stop the ticking I heard *inside his head* which told us both he could blast my brains out and nobody would be the wiser and he'd have the car, no questions asked—

"Twenty thousand," Jaime offered.

My outrage mixed with relief. If he were going to kill me, he'd never make an offer. On the other hand—

"It's a half-million dollar car!" I protested.

"At auction. On a good day. For a car with legitimate papers, bill of sale, license and registration—"

"Fifty thousand," I countered quickly.

"Thirty-five," Jaime said.

"Cash?"

"Right in the office there," Jaime agreed.

"Deal," I told him.

Jaime started for the door next to the big garage door—his "office," which was really just a room with a hotplate and mattress. As rich as Jaime must have been...again, not my idea of *Lifestyles of the Rich and Famous.*

Suddenly, Jaime stopped on his short walk, as though he'd changed his mind and decided on the gun again.

"You're too reckless," Jaime said sincerely.

"I'm very careful," I protested.

The man was pissing me off, and my hand was in my pocket now— three steps forward, one button-click and a lunge—

"You aren't doing this for the money," he said.

"Of course I am."

"You're doing it for the thrill."

Blood rose to my face. I hated Jaime more than I'd ever hated him right then.

"I can deal with greed," Jaime said. "The other stuff..." Jaime shook his head, the weight of the world on his shoulders. He shuffled into the office.

I felt like kicking the Ferrari, putting a fifty-grand dent in the thing—

Jaime returned with a shopping bag full of cash. I took a glance. It wouldn't do to count it there in front of the man; Jaime would consider it an insult. It would be the right amount anyway. Jaime wasn't that kind of asshole.

"Keys?" he asked.

I handed them to him.

"Now get out of here," he said.

"I need a ride."

"Take the bus."

I laughed, but he wasn't kidding.

"Better yet, Uber. That's what all you kids use now, isn't it?" he asked. "Uber?" he cackled.

I stared, shifting the money to my left hand, freeing the right—

"Just call it in from down the block if you don't mind," Jaime added casually, as if he had no idea how close to death he was at that point.

I turned and took a walk, like Alan Ladd did at the beginning of *Shane* (1953), before he was forced to go all Tarantino on the bad guys. L-O-T-F-A-D. "Live On To Fight Another Day"—that's my motto.

I didn't care. I refused to care. I had thirty-five thousand dollars in my pocket. The moon winked at me. I wasn't afraid. I'd driven a Ferrari that night. I was not ashamed. I wasn't a star but you couldn't prove that if you looked at my face, or in my pocket—the one with the money, not the knife—and besides, that not being a star thing was just a matter of time.

CHAPTER 4

Records show George Landon filled his seven-year-old Chrysler 300 with gas in Babcock, Wisconsin, just ten miles west of Nekoosa, the home of Millie and Marston Baker, Julie Baker's father and mother. A fifty-year-old private detective out of Minneapolis, an ex-cop, Landon was considered a "straight-arrow guy," a "solid citizen," and a "good-ol' boy" by friends and colleagues.

"The fact was, he had to make a living," his best friend and chief bowling rival Ned Heller told investigators later, "but George would've done it for free if he could. Investigations, I mean. He considered it doing people a favor, putting their minds at ease. These people lost their daughter and the Hollywood cops weren't finding her, so George jumped in to help. The fact they were paying him for it didn't change George's thinking on the matter."

Credit card records show Landon took I-90 west to Minnesota, then I-35 south to Des Moines, I-80, I-75, I-70 at Denver, then I-15 right into Los Angeles. It was spring and the northern Rocky Mountain route only took him three days, stopping twice overnight at modestly priced chain motels. Nothing unusual about the trip stood out in the public record or among George Landon's private notes when they were finally found.

Once in L.A., Landon checked into a run-down but overpriced tourist motel on the outskirts of Hollywood.

"A fixture since the 50s, considered haunted," Landon wrote in his journal.

The next day, May 15, according to that same journal, George Landon went to see Julie Baker's roommate, "Miss A" in Landon's notes.

"Nothing more to add to the police report," Landon noted in a meticulous hand. "Last heard from JB/RR on April 10. Text message. 'Not home for dinner.' Did not reappear. No more calls/texts/no sign of return to the apartment. Miss A filed missing persons 1 wk. later. No idea of enemies. Known associates: Lowanna Xanderson, Freddy Weaver, Jack C. Cunningham, Clyde (last name unkn.). No known problems, issues. Computer in police custody. Phone whereabouts unkn. Does not ring in apt."

It is believed "JB/RR" referred to "Julie Baker" and her stage-name, "Rayna Rourke."

Everyone who knew George Landon agreed he was a "people person." In an investigation, he'd lean toward "shoe leather" police work rather than electronics surveillance, phone records, GPS, fingerprints or DNA. Of course, some of this was out of necessity; the LAPD wasn't likely to share information—their reputation on that was clear.

But that didn't mean George Landon wasn't without resources. To his surprise, the GPS on Julie's phone was still active, which led him to a particular corner in the heart of the Sunset Strip. He dialed her number. The traffic was light, but he still heard no ringtone, no vibration, no answer. Below his feet was a storm-drain. He knelt to the pavement and dialed again, ear to the drain. Still no sound. People walked by, taking no notice. This was "The Strip," where hipsters came to "be"—nothing would shock them, Landon discovered. If Julie's phone was down in the sewer system it would take a court order and somebody with a stronger stomach than he had to go down there looking for it. And what could be on it? A message, a phone number? Landon had already checked the phone records and had run down most of them.

He shook his head and stepped into the nearest ten establishments— bar, dress shop, sandwich shop, nightclub, restaurant. He flashed Julie's photograph and mentioned both names— Julie Baker and Rayna Rourke— but only got headshakes for his trouble.

"She might have lost her phone in the street over there. Down the drain," Landon suggested. Still no response. "Or somebody might have tossed a phone down there—did you see that happen, maybe? About six weeks ago?" No reaction there, either.

George Landon wasn't surprised. This was par for the course, whether it was Wisconsin, Chicago or this section of West Hollywood bordering Beverly Hills.

At least that's what he tried to tell himself. This wouldn't have a good outcome, his bones told him. Julie had just disappeared into thin air. She wasn't a runaway, she wasn't in any trouble; she was just another good-looking young person seeking fame, fortune and a career in a business that seemed attractive on the outside but everyone knew was as filthy as sin underneath.

Landon checked his watch. He had a little time; Freddy Weaver's acting class didn't start till seven-thirty and it was only five. He shifted down to Hollywood Boulevard, past the Roosevelt Hotel...he slowed. A prostitute tried to get into the Chrysler but the door was locked. Landon waved her away and tried not to run over her. He pulled into a side-street, parked in a lot and strolled up to the boulevard. He'd be a tourist for awhile.

Across the street was the Chinese Theatre with its footprints. Tourists from all over the world walked past on the Walk of Fame, pointing out the plaques to each other, taking pictures. Landon took a deep breath, enjoying it all—the crowds, the activity, the energy, the diversity. Minneapolis had its charms, but nothing like this.

A double-decker tour-bus passed, and the guide on the speaker pointed out the Roosevelt itself.

"Whatever you do, go in there and scare yourselves," the guide told the tourists. "It's haunted like crazy. Ghosts, people! Ghosts! Montgomery Cliff's in there. Marilyn Monroe, too. Carole Lombard. Old Hollywood lives on. Don't believe me, check it out for yourselves, but don't blame me if you choke on your steak or fall down an elevator shaft or get thrown off the roof!" The guide cackled wickedly as the bus continued on down the boulevard.

George Landon smiled to himself and went into the hotel. He wasn't a student of architecture, or nostalgic himself much, or even knew anything about the history of Hollywood, but he recognized this place was worth a look around. He also always wondered if he wasn't related to Michael Landon in any way. Someday, when he was truly retired, he planned to look into that.

"Or maybe I'll ask his ghost," Landon apparently told his wife on the phone when he called her later that night.

There's no evidence he saw any ghosts, however.

"If you're related to anybody famous," his partner Larry Gregg had once teased him, "it's *Alf* Landon."

Later, when the charm of the hotel and Grauman's Chinese and the Hollywood/Highland Entertainment Complex had worn off—*nice mall but still just a mall*—and he'd had a half-decent hotdog and fries—the Bakers in Wisconsin wouldn't want to spring for Musso and Frank on the expense account, Landon decided—he reclaimed his car and drove the mile to Freddy Weaver's acting class. He arrived forty-five minutes early and caught Freddy alone, apparently waking from a nap. After he'd introduced himself and been invited in, Landon looked around a little.

"Hiding it but living in the studio," Landon wrote in his notes. "Not up to code. Not concerned nor surprised that a detective from Wisconsin was looking for one of his students. Seemed sympathetic but he's an actor— might be a performance."

Six months later, Freddy Weaver made this formal statement: "Yes, I spoke to that detective. He was looking for Rayna Rourke, who I was grooming for big things, *huge* things. Quite a talent. Quite...a...talent..."

CHAPTER 5

The Godfather (1972). One of my favorites. Everybody likes it. I've seen it ten times. Why? Some people claim it's because of the fantasy aspect: "Wouldn't it be cool to be able to just 'whack' somebody if they pissed you off?'" Yeah, that's true, it would be cool, but what most people won't acknowledge is... it's that way *now!* If you're just the least bit careful about it, you can pretty much do anything you like to anyone you want, can't you? And nobody gives a damn. Watch your rich people, watch your politicians, look at your Arab princes, check out your cops for that matter. Oh, yeah, occasionally somebody gets caught on a cell-phone or a surveillance camera or something, but most of the time—we're talking 99% here—*nothing happens, nobody knows.*

No, the reason *The Godfather* (1972) is so popular is because it's about *family.* It's the family I never had, the one I longed for and still do. People who'd do anything for you, not because you deserve it or anything, but because you're *family.* I'm starting to cry just thinking about it.

It was a *Halloween* movie—I don't remember which one—but it was definitely *Halloween* (1978 to ten years from now), with Mike Myers stalking people, which was exciting, but not as exciting as sneaking in to see the movies with my little brother and sister—I don't remember which ones—none of us were old enough to be seeing that level of bloodshed but what are you going to do? The heart wants what it wants. Afterwards, we stood outside in the cold waiting forever for the Skullys to pick us up. When they finally came they honked like we hadn't been out there shivering in the cold for hours waiting. My little brother and sister ran to the car and jumped in; I took my time, playing passive-aggressive even at that young age, taking my sweet time, giving the two little ones a chance to spill the beans, they were so excited: "We saw *Halloween!* It scared the bejesus out of us," forgetting we'd been especially forbidden to see that movie on account of a history of nightmares my little sister was afflicted with.

Immediately, Mack and Rose started screaming about how we'd disobeyed their orders while they cuffed my siblings about the head, which gave me second thoughts about jumping in the car to suffer the same abuse—hesitation enough for the grownup Skullys to slam the car shut and screech off without me, leaving me to freeze to death in the winter the entire night, dodging the night-watchman, curling up under some decorative landscaping. In the morning they came back to again honk the horn and this time I hustled quickly to the warm car—

"You'd *better* run!" father Skully shouted while mother Skully laughed her head off.

"Looks like our little man froze his little wiener off!" she howled.

Later, I got what was referred to as a "severe correction," completing my humiliation and preparing me for a life in show business.

The audition was in one of those rental places in what used to be an office building or rehearsal space or 99-seat theatre—they're all over Hollywood. I took the latest time-slot I could get—you want to go last—they always cast the last person they see. So I walk in and there's a big waiting room with a hundred actors crammed into it, sitting around dressed to impress, and lots of little rooms surrounding them, tiny offices sort of. There's no receptionist—that might cost money—just a sign that tells you to go to your smart-phone and sign in on their website and let them know you're there and then they'll call you—about as impersonal as it gets.

The movie was called *Terror Magic*, or *The Magic Terror*—I've forgotten already. They wanted me to read for the part of Derek, some kind of sadistic freak who lured hot young girls to his mansion with the promise of pulling something out of a hat, tempting them with money, getting their tops off then drowning them in his swimming pool, blah blah blah, making them disappear.

"Me? I am a magician" was my first line, but when I said it the producer-director and his idiot girlfriend-assistant burst out laughing.

"What?" I asked.

"It's muh-JISH-un," the producer-director jerk corrected, like I was an idiot five-year-old.

"What I say?" I shot back, getting testy now—I'd sat in that damn waiting room *for almost an hour!*

"You said 'MA-juck-can,'" the little bitch aide gloated, chuckling again. "Magic Can. What's that? It's magician."

I pictured both their heads mounted on a spike. It wouldn't take but a minute, and I could take their little purring mini-camera with me on the way out.

But then I decided to go another way. Drawing on all my resources, particularly P-E-A-C-E, exhaling, I began again, but they'd already knocked me off my feed, kicked me off my game. I pressed on, nevertheless, with incredible courage if I do say so myself but they kept laughing at every little sputter or word I mispronounced—this was a cold reading, mind you, and okay, so maybe my public school education wasn't exactly first-rate, okay? I tried to tell them I had dyslexia a little bit and a touch of A-D-D and sometimes I didn't read things too well first time through, but they weren't a bit sympathetic, so I ended up throwing their idiot script back into their stupid faces and marching out, except I couldn't get the door open right away which made me even madder and got them laughing all the harder. Needless to say, I slammed the door *really* hard which finally got everybody's attention.

Not that I care, I told myself as I marched up the hill to my room. Once home, I checked my social media sites—I'm a member of a dozen of them, all kinds, but mostly the ones with young, attractive women. I picked a feisty-looking little raven with a half million followers—Helen Majors—a go-getter, hungry, new in town and anxious to make her mark quickly before her money ran out. Naive. Trusting. Dark. Ethnic. Built like the proverbial "house o' shit." We met at a coffee shop and hit it right off. She was hooked on the fact I was a talent manager, so she didn't have any complaints about us going back to my place at the Arbuckle. She had heard about it, and it put her off a little, but when I explained my house in the hills had been red-tagged for earthquake repairs and mudslides and forest fires and this was only temporary, she accepted the lie—she was just that horny or that desperate, or she was a hooker in disguise, always a danger in the big city. As for me, let's say I was entirely satisfied by the encounter, and it totally took the edge off the earlier humiliation of that audition. Did I mention?—I'm the expert at humiliation. I've been through it all. You can't throw *nothing* at me I haven't seen before.

Afterwards, as I walked over to Freddy Weaver's acting class, I realized I didn't need them. *I'd make my own damn movies,* that's what I'd do. I'd get Rayna to be in them, too, and we'd make a fortune and screw the hell out of the rest of the world. By the time I'd made it to class, I'd figured it all out again, and was back on an even keel. Scripts are for wimps, anyway. The *real* actors ignore the script and make it up as they go.

I walked into Freddy Weaver's just as he was making an introduction.

"Joining us tonight is Mr. George Landon. He'll be observing, that's all. Welcome, Mr. Landon."

Right away, I spotted the guy as a cop.

CHAPTER 6

Larry Gregg had a funny feeling about this one. Technically George Landon was not his partner but they worked together often. They were both detectives, and both had been on the job for years with the Minneapolis Police Department. Both were middle aged, technically retired, Larry slightly younger at 45, both married. Larry's two kids were off at college; George's were just finishing.

Gregg got the call from George's wife saying Landon had "gone off on some crazy mission to Los Angeles to find a girl."

That wasn't unusual. In fact, nothing about it was unusual. Except George Landon never came back. That was just wrong. George's wife knew it. Larry Gregg knew it. Something had to be done. George Landon was a good friend.

Gregg didn't have much to go on. Landon left a trail of sorts, but pretty low-tech, nothing as smart and sophisticated as uploading his files and notes to the internet, or emailing them to himself. Larry Gregg wasn't even sure when he started if his friend *had* an email account. It turned out he did, but didn't use it much. He had a phone, too, but was either not sophisticated enough or too paranoid to turn the settings to "find." It would take a court order and a damn good reason to track his phone and Larry Gregg didn't have either, just a wife's worry.

After checking in with Julie's parents, who filled him in on the assignment they'd given Landon and assuring him they hadn't heard in weeks either, Gregg hit the road, taking the same path, I-90 first, then I-35 south.

He stopped at every filling station and diner where Landon had used his credit card, and quizzed the employees about the photograph of Landon that Gregg showed them. Some remembered him a little, others not. Some lied about it, saying they recognized him—that was par for the course; people just tell you what you want to hear sometimes.

The clerk at the first motel, on the road past Des Moines, was more convincing.

"Yeah, I remember him. Cop, wasn't he?" the clerk smiled, pleased with himself. "Like you," he told Gregg.

"Private detective," Gregg corrected. The kid was twenty, farm-boy, an obvious police buff, which could be a blessing or a curse. He'd be willing to cooperate, but too anxious to "help"—embellishing, overstating, puffing up the importance of minor issues.

"He checked in about oh-ten-hundred—this was like three weeks ago..."

The clerk checked the register—

"The eighth of the month," Gregg told him. The clerk found the entry and turned the book to the detective. It was George Landon's signature all right. "Can you give me that same room?" Gregg asked.

The clerk checked.

"Sure," he said. "But there've been a dozen people in and out of there since then."

"That's okay," Gregg assured the man.

"You think he hid something in there or left a message?"

"I don't know."

"Or DNA? You think there's DNA?" the clerk asked eagerly.

"No," Gregg replied sharply, his patience wearing thin. "Just give me the key, please."

"You want to know if he made any calls from that room or ran up any other charges, like if he saw a pay-movie on TV or something?"

"Good thinking, kid," Gregg replied, regretting the "kid" part of it—this wasn't some 30s *film noir*, after all. "You find anything, you just let me know when I check out tomorrow morning, all right?"

"Roger," the clerk whispered conspiratorially.

Alone in his room, despite the absurdity of it, Larry Gregg *did* check for evidence of George Landon having been there. He looked under the bed and under the mattress, and behind things. He rifled through the little pad of note-paper—that's where Gregg figured *he'd* write an SOS if he needed it. He also thumbed through the pages of the *Bible* and the *Book of Mormon*—

"Where's the *Koran* and the *Bhagavad Gita*?" Gregg joked to himself. "Racist motel."

There was no sign of George Landon anywhere, but Gregg refused to give up on an idea brewing in the back of his mind: maybe George Landon never made it to Los Angeles. Gregg had watched *Detour* (1945) late one night recently on some obscure TV station. Gregg didn't remember much about it except how good it was, and how sharp the dialogue was, and (SPOILER ALERT) the fact it was about a guy who died driving his car cross-country, then the hitchhiker with him took his wallet and his car and pretended to be him all the way to LA.

Landon would have called Gregg "nutsville" for bringing it up, but it sounded plausible to Gregg. Landon's wife had said he'd called from Hollywood as late as last week, but nobody had ever checked those calls for the exact location, and besides, they could have been made under duress. Landon could have been kidnapped. He could be dead now.

The similarity to Hitchcock's *Psycho* (1960) wasn't lost on Gregg, either—creepy desk-clerk, detective looking for a particular missing woman. Could George Landon have gotten the Martin Balsam treatment on the stairs? Gregg stood and checked for peepholes, cameras, a stray light shining in from somewhere. He reminded himself not to do anything in this motel room he wouldn't want seen all over the internet—

That was the difference between Landon and Gregg, and why they worked so well together when they worked as a team, which was seldom. Landon was a "just the facts, ma'am" shoe-leather guy; Gregg had the imagination to come up with all sorts of crazy, whacked-out scenarios which seldom panned out (well, *never*) but Gregg's oddball notions did always strangely seemed to put the pair on some kind of track, a direction they wouldn't have come up with otherwise, which almost always led to success.

The next morning the clerk made a point to catch Gregg before he could drive off without bothering to check out.

"No phone calls, no movies," the clerk told the detective, who had to remind himself what the kid was talking about.

"Oh...okay, thanks," Gregg told the eager buff. Gregg drove off in his Buick, keeping an eye on the rear-view mirror, wondering, then dismissing the idea. Julie Baker had taken the bus, then the train into LA. She'd never stopped in that motel, though he couldn't speak for all the other young beauties this psychopath of a hotel employee had stashed in the attic—

Gregg crushed the gas pedal and roared onto the interstate. If he didn't find George Landon in Los Angeles, he'd definitely come back here...maybe see some justice done.

CHAPTER 7

I would have loved to have attempted the Zoroastrian Tower of Silence ceremony on her. The water tower on the roof would have been perfect. The Zoroastrians considered a dead body unclean, which I don't agree with at all—it depends on what you do with it. But to the Zoroastrians any contact of a body to the Earth is a pollution of the planet—a "putrefaction"—so they put a dead body up on a high tower to be exposed to the sun and to have its flesh ripped away by scavenging birds to be taken to higher nests, and hopefully the birds didn't drop anything on the ground either.

The water tower wouldn't be the same of course—it would be a toss-up who would get to Helen Majors first—rats, squirrels, pigeons, flies. Not too many vultures in this part of Hollywood, just the human kind, ha ha.

That was her name—Helen Majors—it said so on her photo ID, the kind they give you at the DMV if you're too old or too young to drive. My guess is her name was really something Mexican. I hadn't really wanted somebody that young, or that Hispanic, but she surprised me, pleasantly. I'm white, okay, so naturally I tend to my own kind, and blonde and buxom, both top and bottom, skinny waist—that's my thing: "Old School"—though a slender, perky-breasted one will do in the dark—

Hell, I like them all—I admit it. I can't help it. Which is why it hurts me so much to do what I do sometimes. I can't help that either.

Helen had it in all the right places, I had to give her that. A lot of solid flesh on those bones, mottled with just enough fat—perfect. Didn't taste like chicken. Duck. Ha!

Excarnation. Google it. Tearing the flesh off human bones—when dead, of course—we're not animals. They did it all over the world and still do, standard procedure in some cultures. They did it to knights and saints and kings and demigods, so it's not a bad thing, trust me. It's religious.

First you have to get a good knife; that's the most important thing. Get yourself a good sharp knife—a couple different ones, too, in different sizes, and a cleaver—and I mean sharp, the kind that makes you bleed just looking at it. And you'll need a sharpener, and don't forget to use it, and often. Buy some sheets of plastic for neatness sake—you want to get that security deposit back. Then it's over to one of those big box stores like Target or Walmart or Home Depot for a half-dozen large plastic storage bins. Cheap and easy and you don't have time or money or space for a freezer that large.

Dry ice? Forget it. If your containers aren't vented right they can explode, not to mention how you're going to have to be super-careful about handling dry ice. Buying it can be a hassle, too—you don't want to be explaining why you need that much every day or two. Go to your nearest convenience store and purchase regular ice. No fuss, no muss—they'll peg you as a heavy drinker who likes it on the rocks, which in this society is considered far more acceptable than cannibalism for some reason.

The point of all this flesh-eating of course is to obtain power, stolen from the victim, digested nicely. Their spiritual potentiality becomes yours—simple as that. Try it sometime.

CHAPTER 8

Larry Gregg checked in on the Los Angeles Police Department and spoke to the detectives. He expected the usual razzing and wasn't disappointed. Cops and private eyes don't get along, just like in the movies and crime books.

Gregg didn't care. He'd been a cop himself and if it helped smooth the way with LA's finest, he was willing to take a little flack. He also wasn't hesitant to play the "ex-cop" card to its full value. Sure, Minneapolis wasn't Los Angeles, but there was still a relationship there even the most hardened cop in the Ramparts or Hollywood Division had to acknowledge. And the fact Gregg was looking for one of their own, George Landon—another cop, retired—helped to further dull the barbs...a little.

On the other hand, the police detectives didn't give a holy damn about Julie Baker, aka Rayna Rourke. They had her down as a prostitute, and nobody cares about a missing prostitute— anywhere in the world.

"Why do you think she was a prostitute?" Gregg had to ask.

"To make money?" a wag commented from the other side of the room.

"Low morals?" another chimed in.

They all laughed.

"I mean," Gregg smiled patiently, "what makes you *think* she was a prostitute?"

A police detective came over, rolling his considerable shoulders and hips like John Wayne in *Red River* (1948), ready to teach little Montgomery Cliff a thing or two. He pointed to the line on Julie Baker's missing-persons card, "Profession," and the typed-in response: "Actress." Below that, in parentheses: "Prostitute."

"What makes you think that?" Gregg challenged. "Had she ever been picked up?"

The police detective took another look at the file and shook his head.

"So just 'cause she's young and attractive and an actress, that makes her a hooker?" Gregg wanted to know, incredulous.

"Uh huh," came the reply.

"So Meryl Streep, Maggie Smith, Dame Edith Evans and Glenn Close are all prostitutes?"

The cop stared.

"What about Julie Andrews?" Gregg pressed on. "You telling me Mary *fucking* Poppins did tricks on the side?"

"None of those actresses are young..." the cop replied calmly, "and Dame Edith Evans is deceased, by the way. Our condolences to the family."

Gregg walked out in disgust. The LAPD hadn't looked into Julie Baker's disappearance for more than a minute. "There are a million stories in the big city" and Julie's wasn't one of them—at least not one they were interested in pursuing. Neither had they looked into the disappearance of George Landon.

"We got the missing person's report, we got his picture, vitals, license number, prints—he shows up anywhere on the radar, we'll let his next-of-kin know. We got that number here, right on the card," the police told him.

"That's it?" Gregg had asked.

"He's a big-shot detective like you, right? He can handle himself, can't he? Maybe he just decided to get lost in La-La Land where it's seventy degrees at some point every day. It's what I'd do if I lived in some hell-hole of a city in the Midwest like..." the cop looked at the information card like he'd forgotten the place—

"Minneapolis," Gregg informed him.

"Whatever," the cop had replied.

Gregg knew what he had to do: *look to the movies.*

In this case *Klute* (1971) came to mind, starring Donald Sutherland as the title character, detective from the boonies, like Gregg, a hint of Canadian accent (like Gregg, too, but more south: Minnesota), lost in the big city trying to find someone important, forced to take a long look at the seedier side of things.

Yeah, Larry Gregg could play that role. He knew his limitations, but he was born for that role. And if need be, he could fall in love with a hooker all right...especially if she looked like Jane Fonda (fifty years ago)...or Julie Baker.

CHAPTER 9

A person's bones use up about 15% of his/her body weight. I figured Helen Majors weighed about 150 pounds, which would put her bones at 22 and a half pounds, give or take. *You* do the math. Not that heavy, but try carrying that load up a creaky old steel ladder and pushing it into a water-tank. The weight was only half of it; the awkwardness of uncut, unbroken bones doubled the challenge.

I waited until about 10 o'clock in the evening. That was late enough to not be noticed in the dark and early enough not to be suspicious. I got a box of large compostable garbage bags at the same place I bought the plastic tubs and used three of them. I carried all three in one trip up the ladder; next time I'll smarten up and do it one at a time. I skipped the elevator—too dangerous—somebody could catch you going the wrong way and you'd be going down and they'd be stuck staring at your green plastic bags and wondering why you hadn't tossed them down the chute—there's one on every floor. "What's in the bags?" they'd say and you'd have to lie about it and give them some story, which might have holes in it.

I had planned to kill Helen if she turned out to be a hooker, which she wasn't, just a poor, pathetic lost soul, which made me mad, too, so I did it anyway. It would have been okay to keep her around awhile, take advantage, use her for a while. Maybe next time. Her real name was Elena Mejia, I discovered after going through her purse more thoroughly. I wondered if that name was already taken by another actress or if she'd just changed it to disguise her ethnicity. I should have asked her. Now it was too late.

I got a couple tickets to a free Academy screening on Wilshire, the Sam Goldwyn Theater, which impressed the hell out of Rayna. That part was easy; getting reservations for before the show at The Porch on Abbot Kinney in Venice is like climbing Everest but guess what? I did it anyway. I'm already a mover and a shaker in this town when it comes to that sort of thing—no two ways about it.

The food was what you'd expect: tasty, tiny portions of meat and vegetables entirely unobtainable in any grocery store in the continental United States, creatively tarted up with odd combinations of spices. They insisted on describing every ingredient in every dish, which also impressed Rayna to no end. She had the marinated Castelvetrano Olives with melon passato, crispy garlic, basil and white anchovies. I ate prawns, crabs and calamari and told the waiter to "keep 'em comin.'"

I picked up a Lexus for the occasion and—against my religious beliefs—did the valet parking thing.

Then it happened. Right place at the right time. Izzy Clurman, producer, sat at a table with a few friends, one female, two male. The woman was older, clearly not his date, but belonging to another older man—studio executive, no doubt—though I didn't recognize him. They had a better table, but not by much. They made casual conversation, chuckling more than laughing, having a good time, but there was clearly something on Clurman's mind—Rayna.

He started by sneaking glances at her, then he made no bones about it—he stared. Rayna, situated facing slightly away from him, had no idea, but I could clearly see he was interested.

R-P-R-T. Overrated by some, underestimated by others. What the commentators neglect to mention is you have to be at the Right Place at the Right Time *and* be ready to seize that moment. It's a three-legged stool. That night, I was sitting pretty.

Next time old dirty fucker Izzy Clurman checked out Rayna, I made sure I caught his eye and gave him a quick grin and a little salute—the "we're both rich and important and of course we need to get along" salute. He returned it.

I stalled another minute or two, stuffed some more seafood into my face and ordered another glass of wine, vintage—I was still holding Ferrari money, after all. I got up and took the walk to the men's room, taking the route past Clurman—

"Good evening, Mr. Clurman," I told him, stopping only long enough pat his shoulder—

He took the bait, excusing himself, following me—

"Do I know you?" he asked in the men's room, genuinely not sure.

"I don't think we've met," I answered, handing him my business card.

"Oh...an agent," he said, reading the card like I'd just pasted a wet, smelly dog-turd into his hand.

I slipped my own hand to the sharpened eight-incher in my pocket— British steel, ambidextrous thumb activation—prepared to stab first, low, then upward—spill his guts right on the blue and pink tile—

"Who's the girl?" he asked with slightly more respect. "Client? Girlfriend? Wife?"

I smiled. He was hooked. Prepared to do business. *Kiss my ass, bitch.*

"She's an actress," I replied.

He liked that answer, the pig.

"Been in anything?" he asked.

"Not yet," I answered.

"You didn't answer the first question," he remarked, that little smirk at the edge of his mouth expanding.

"She's my client," I told him. "Prettiest girl in Hollywood."

He laughed—that was a bridge too far—can't bullshit a bullshitter—

"Lots of pretty girls in Hollywood," he remarked.

"This one can act," I told him convincingly.

He shrugged, not so interested in that.

"How about if I introduce you?" I suggested.

"I'm with some people," he answered.

"I'll call you tomorrow."

He shook his head. The last thing in the world he was going to do was give me his phone number, no matter how hard he was for Rayna. But he pocketed *my* card, giving it a final finger snap.

"I'll call you," he said. "Now I'm going back to my table and you're going back to your table and we won't speak again, understand?"

"I get it—"

"Ever," he said.

Then he was gone—

We went to the movie, which was garbage, something about a woman feeling guilty about her husband dying or her children dying or some shit, in Eastern Europe during WWII or WWI, I couldn't tell which. I was still thinking about Izzy Clurman and how to play that angle. He'd seemed genuinely hot for Rayna but tomorrow he might have second thoughts and what if he never called? I could track him down at the studio—I'd have to figure out which one—maybe we'd need to stake him out, throw Rayna in front of his Bentley or some crazy thing—

"What a beautiful film," Rayna glowed, taking my arm as we walked to the car afterwards—the Goldwyn doesn't even have valet parking, for crying out loud—

"Gorgeous," I replied, faking it. Like a lot of other women in the audience, and some of the men, Rayna had cried through a big hunk of the film. I couldn't see why.

Before we got to the parking lot, she held me closer and whispered into my ear: "You want to go back to my place, Jack?"

I shivered. I froze. I hadn't expected this. Instinctively, my hand went to my pocket and the forged steel instrument—

Of all the fucking times to bring this up, Rayna had to pick this night, unlike all the other nights, when I'd made a connection to Izzy *fucking* Clurman—

"My roommate's not going to be there," she cooed. "She's on location..."

I still didn't answer.

"It's been a lovely evening," Rayna tried, sounding a little needy. "A wonderful dinner and a beautiful movie..."

She was trying, I had to give the kid that. Next she was going to say, "I just want to show my appreciation," which would have been a nice gesture as well. I could see she also felt guilty about going with Lowanna Xanderson for her agent, and meant to make it up to me. At least she was putting it out there on a transactional basis without all that lovey-dovey stuff. Tit for tat, and she had a nice pair, I had to admit. The night before I would have jumped at the chance and nailed her but good, but the Izzy thing got to me. Not that I cared, not that I'd sell her to the well-known producer for a dime less or a dime more if we "did it" or were "doing it," or had been a couple for decades, but people's feelings get in the way, don't they?—not mine, but other people's— Izzy might not like it. He might not care now, but down the line he might, maybe a lot, and with millions at stake, why take the chance?

I blipped the Lexus open and we got in. I still hadn't answered Rayna's question. It looked like she was going to cry again, like she had in the movie. I don't like it when women cry. It makes me angry. Girls make me do things when they cry like that. Things they don't like either.

"Ours is a business relationship," I told her when we both sat in the car, before I started it up. "Whatever feelings you have for me, you push them way down deep inside yourself and use those for your career, and for your acting, understand?"

Rayna nodded. She understood completely: I desperately wanted her but I was sacrificing my own desires for her greater good. She respected me for that. She loved me for it. Poor kid.

I let her off and made sure she got into her apartment okay, then I went back to mine at the Arbuckle. I finished filling out an application to the State of Oregon for an original birth certificate. I vowed to finally establish my relationship with the Skullys once and for all.

Fight Club (1999)—that's what it was like growing up with the Skullys. "You don't talk about Fight Club," except it was "You don't talk about the Skullys." I knew if I ever said a word about the horror that took place in the compound, there would be hell to pay.

Second rule of "Skully Club" was "nobody wants you, nobody gives a shit about you, you are a worthless piece of crap." Never mind that's three rules.

(Note on *Fight Club* (1999): brilliant film, SPOILERS—tremendous use of an unreliable narrator—I love that shit. Preys on the audience's ludicrous expectations and the conventions of film itself, see *Sixth Sense* (1999) and *The Usual Suspects* (1995). Morons who think *Fight Club* (1999) is great the first half and "the wheels come off in the last half" have no brains and no souls. IMO.)

Did I mention the Skullys were armed to the teeth: rifles, pistols, shotguns, knives, hatchets, spears? They were ready for war, against whom they weren't very specific, but I won't go into that—you know who you are.

One night when I was about ten I was awakened by tense whispers.

"Somebody's on the property!" was what I heard, but I can't be sure. I heard the clatter of guns then, and knives being strapped on. I dared to creep to the window and look out to the snowbound majesty of our front property. Mother and father Skully ran into view in their nightclothes—they both sported "union suits," the kind of underwear you only see in old black and white cartoons. Mack had a belt of ammo magazines hanging down over his shoulder and an AR-15 in his arms. Rose followed with an arsenal cradled against her bosom, bless her heart. They ran out into the crunching snow shouting curses at the interloper until they disappeared into the woods and I couldn't see anymore through the fogged-up window of my room.

A volley of shots followed—a full magazine of thirty rounds? That's a guess. Oregon limits magazines to three rounds for bird hunting. For large game it's five. Shooting humans? *No* limit at all—"nice little civilization you got here—too bad if something happened to it"—but I don't think even my foster parents went more than thirty rounds.

The body was unrecognizable but we all knew who they'd killed by process of elimination: Hector. He was nine or ten and loved to read. He'd only been with the clan a couple of weeks. Right off we knew he was different. He was a sleep-walker. He'd be up all hours of the night, headed for the refrigerator, turning on the TV, setting out into the woods, but not the outhouse. After the first few nights, we were all under strict orders to lock all the doors and keep the key from Hector. If we had to pee, there were jars available.

I guess somebody forgot to lock one of the doors. Rose blamed Mack and Mack blamed Rose, but I'm not sure either of them did it. It might have been me, just to see what would happen.

There wasn't much left of Hector's body after a dozen high-powered shots rifled through it. Father wasn't much of a shot, but he did okay that night. The ground was too frozen to bury the kid, so we dragged him out into the woods a half-mile in the freezing cold, trailing bloody snow—it didn't matter, nobody would be out there to investigate—and left him for the ravens, wolves, bears, whoever needed a solid meal. Call it a form of excarnation, except I imagine the wolves ate the bones, too.

"That's the way of life, after all," Mack Skully announced by way of an epitaph before we walked the distance back to the house, just the two of us. I remember the moment well, a rare bond between father and son. I never liked Hector much anyway.

I thought of all that as I placed the application in the envelope and sealed it shut. I hoped the State of Oregon would finally solve the mystery of my birth and permanently and irrevocably separate myself from my parental impostors, Mack and Rose Skully.

The application was $25. I could afford that. It would take 3-5 weeks. I could wait. After that, armed with the real dope, my birth-name and my birthplace, and hopefully the name of my parents, attending physician, a hospital location, I could finally embark on the quest of my lifetime, to find out who I was and where I came from. I'd find my real mother and real father, perhaps brothers and sisters.

CHAPTER 10

"If I called the cops every time somebody just took off without settling the bill," the motel clerk told Larry Gregg, "that's all I would do all day."

"You didn't think it was unusual, a guy just disappears like that and leaves all his things?"

"Happens sometimes," the clerk shrugged. "He looked like a big boy. He looked like he could handle himself."

"You kept his belongings?" Gregg asked.

"Sure. I'm not a monster."

"Let's see 'em," Gregg demanded.

The motel clerk thought about that.

"Okay," he said finally. "You can look, but you can't take them. They're *his* property and as far as I know, you're not authorized."

Gregg knew that wasn't the real reason.

"It would save you some trouble to give me his stuff," Gregg suggested. "I'd get it all back to his wife, whose property it *actually* is, saving you the cops sniffing around and asking questions and missing persons and 'are you all up to code?' and inspections and smoke detectors—I don't know what-all the statutes are around here—"

"Okay, okay," the clerk said. "The stuff's in the back. You gotta stand right there so I can keep an eye on you while I get it. It's a couple boxes and a suitcase."

"Go," Gregg told the man. "I'll wait here."

Gregg watched the clerk go into a back room, a tiny office stacked to the ceiling with boxes and suitcases. *People leave things here a lot*, it occurred to Gregg. The clerk made a couple trips—two boxes and a suitcase just as he'd said. He hadn't hesitated, either, which made Gregg think the man had already gone through Detective George Landon's things.

A quick look suggested nothing of value was left, except for one priceless item: Landon's case-book...his notes. Gregg rifled through it like a kid at Christmas.

"That's what you were looking for?" the motel clerk asked.

"Bingo," Gregg answered. "You want to rent me a room?" he asked.

"Nothing would thrill me more."

"Can you give me that same room?" Gregg asked.

"Why?" the clerk asked with great suspicion.

Gregg didn't tell him. He didn't have to. Cash explained it all, and the clerk relinquished all of Landon's things as well. As he had in the motel in Iowa, Larry Gregg checked again for evidence of George Landon having been there. As before, there was no sign.

Gregg went through Landon's things again, keeping the notebook separate. Landon travelled light was about all Gregg could glean—the notebook was the only thing of value. It convinced Gregg that Landon had made it to Hollywood—Gregg recognized the handwriting. The notes concerned the investigation, interviews and thoughts from after he arrived. Unless this was some highly elaborate scheme, the *Detour* scenario was out.

There was a knock at the door.

"Who is it?" Gregg asked, hand reflexively going to the small of his back, where he kept a snub-nose .38.

"Hotel manager," Gregg heard. He recognized the clerk's voice. The kid had given himself a promotion.

Gregg opened the door.

"I forgot to tell you something," the clerk said. "I warned your boy-friend about it, too."

"Ha ha, what?"

"Marilyn Monroe fucked a city councilman to death in that room there," he announced, pointing past Gregg.

"Well, good for her," Gregg replied and started to close the door again.

"That's not the warning," the clerk told the detective.

"Listen, I'm sure the rubes are very interested in your little 'Hollywood folk-tales—'"

"He comes back," the clerk interrupted. "She does, too. They appear in this room sometimes. Hundreds have seen them. Your friend might have seen them. There's film. Somebody shot film. A stag film, for smoker parties and stuff. It was the fifties, or the forties, I don't know."

Gregg smiled patiently.

"Thank you for the warning," he said. "I will keep an eye out for them and say hello for you if you like."

The motel clerk turned white and held his hands high.

"Leave me out of it."

Gregg laughed as he closed the door lightly but firmly on the man's nose.

The interview with Julie Baker's roommate went a little better. Gregg found the apartment, standard 50s motel style, doors off an outdoor walkway surrounding a leafy, brown-water swimming pool, half-filled, health hazard.

"Julie Baker?" the young woman asked at the door, face scrunched up like a squeezed lemon. "Never heard of her."

"You may know her as Rayna Rourke?" Gregg tried.

"Hey, what's the deal?" Miss Joan Arento wanted to know. "You didn't come here a couple weeks ago, did you?"

"No, that wasn't me—"

"Asking the same questions about Rayna?"

"That wasn't me," Gregg protested, pulling out a picture of George Landon to show. "See?"

"That's him!" Miss Arento realized. "Okay—you're both about the same age and I see a lot of faces in my line of work—"

"It's okay," Gregg assured the woman. "I understand."

"Did you find Rayna?" Miss Arento wanted to know.

"Not yet," Gregg admitted. "And now we've lost *him*, too." Gregg tapped George Landon's photograph.

The roommate froze, realizing the seriousness of that information.

"He came looking for Rayna, now he's dead, too?"

"I didn't say either one of them was dead," Gregg pointed out, a little peeved. "Why do you say they're dead?"

"I've been around. I read the papers. I watch the news and listen to the radio—"

"Maybe you shouldn't do that."

"Maybe not," the woman agreed.

"May I come in and ask you a few questions?" Gregg tried.

Miss Arento let him in. The place was a shared two-bedroom. Not clean but not messy, either. The occupants didn't have much: a TV, an old couch, a few books. Gregg took as long as he could checking the place out without being rude.

"You want to sit?" Miss Arento challenged.

Gregg sat. He tried to figure out which bedroom belonged to Julie and which was the roommate's. Nothing gave it away.

Miss Arento sat, too, and Gregg peppered her with questions. She didn't have much more to say than what was in George Landon's notes.

Rayna had disappeared without warning. There'd been no contact. "Miss A" had gone to the police after a week. They'd taken Rayna's laptop.

"Who knows what they did with that?" Miss Arento noted. "Probably sold it."

Gregg went down the list of associates.

"Freddy Weaver's a good bet for a serial killer," Miss Arento noted. "He's her acting teacher. Runs an acting school. I'd check him out first."

"Why do you say that?" Gregg asked.

"He's always on the prowl, that's why. Like shooting fish in a barrel. Screws everything in sight. We're all gorgeous, you may have noticed, every one of us."

Gregg blushed. He shrugged. He pretended he hadn't noticed.

"Wherever we came from, we were the prettiest," the roommate went on. "'Go to Hollywood—you're gorgeous,' they said, so we did. Straight from the ghettos and farms—the most beautiful hunks of womanhood you're going to see. Sheep to the slaughter, devoured by predators: phony managers, phony agents, phony friends, fake human beings whose cocks are the only thing straight about them—if you're lucky." She chuckled.

Once again, Gregg went a shade of red.

"You're cute," Miss Arento noted. "You could get some here."

Gregg didn't know if she meant "here in the general area" or "right here, right now—"

"We flock to 'em—anybody who smells of movies," the woman continued. "'Ride me, ride me!' we beckon, so they do—ride us, that is—even though they stink of failure, and death, and big piles of rotting plans."

Miss Arento looked off into the distance. If she'd had a cigarette, she'd have taken a puff right then. Traffic from the street filtered in, angry, honking. Gregg felt he was suddenly in a B-movie from the fifties, a *noir*, tough talk and tougher women. He loved it.

"You ever see *Detour*?" Gregg asked, a sudden thought.

"What's that, a movie?" Miss Arento asked.

"Yeah, it's a movie," Gregg answered.

"You asking me out to a movie?"

Gregg laughed.

"What's so funny about that?" Miss Arento asked, hurt.

"Nothing. Nothing. It's an old movie, before either of us were born, that's all," Gregg explained. "I doubt it's showing anywhere. But I'd love to go to a movie with you some time, except right now I'm on this case—"

"Yeah yeah," Miss Arento said. "Take it easy. I'm not asking you to marry me or anything. Or even fuck me, okay?"

"Could I take a look at Julie's room?" Gregg asked, standing, pointing to one of the bedrooms.

"That's mine," the roommate said wryly. Again, a hint of vamp crept into her voice.

Gregg turned to the other bedroom.

"Could I?"

"Have fun," Miss Arento told him. "It's all yours."

"Thanks."

Gregg hurried into Julie's room and started looking. He would like to have more time, but he figured fifteen minutes was about all the roommate would stand for. There wasn't much to the room—a quarter of an hour would probably do it anyway. As casually as he could make it, checking the bureau first, Gregg glanced up to see if Miss Arento was watching. She was, but then she moved into the kitchen. He heard her washing dishes.

As expected, Julie's room was a disappointment. Her life revolved around acting, with little sign of anything else. A number of screenplays had been printed out from the internet. Even the books she read were adaptations of movies. She'd ordered 500 "headshots," professional photographs—Gregg took a dozen of them and stuck them in his small briefcase. There were no drugs, no condoms, no booze—nothing to indicate Julie was taking advantage of what the big city might offer.

"Might as well have stayed home, pretty girl," Gregg muttered to himself.

At the end of the fifteen minutes, as Gregg predicted, the roommate showed up at the door to nudge him along.

"I'd better go," Gregg said, standing up from checking under the mattress. He walked past Miss Arento and headed for the door.

"Listen," she said, grabbing his arm. "If you find out anything you come back here, okay, and you tell me."

"Yes, of course, I will."

"Okay then," the young woman said, releasing Gregg's arm. "Okay."

Larry Gregg couldn't help thinking of Miss Arento's description of the predators of Hollywood when he faced Freddy Weaver. "Nauseous and depressing," Gregg wrote in his own journal as he listened to the acting guru. In no mood for bullshit, which was the teacher's "go-to" move, Gregg pressed Weaver hard, to the point of threatening him physically.

"Yeah, okay," Freddy Weaver protested, "so I've had affairs with a bunch of actors and actresses. Some of them were students, okay? It's done. It's how it works. A pretty face moves up the food chain—"

"Rayna Rourke?" Gregg wanted to know.

"Yeah, her too," Weaver confessed.

In the wings, listening in, hidden, Jack C. Cunningham's eyes grew wide and his jaw tightened in rage.

"But I didn't hurt her. Why would I hurt her? She was the sweetest piece of ass I've had in a long time."

Jack didn't move. He refused to move. His rage would find itself useful in other ways...

"I don't know where she went," Freddy Weaver whined. "I don't know why she disappeared. It wasn't because of *me*, believe me. I'm a pile of shit in the middle of the sidewalk but I'm not a killer, and no young woman's gonna get a broken heart over the likes of me, believe *that*."

Gregg didn't reply. The guy was clearly telling the truth.

CHAPTER 11

I knew where Rayna was. I was the reason she'd disappeared. She was shacked up in a Brentwood mansion with a producer by the name of Izzy Clurman who I sold her to, or close to it. I thought it would do her career good. I figured he would put her in pictures. He still might, but I was having my doubts. He had her caged up there like Norma Desmond had William Holden trapped in *Sunset Boulevard* (1950) or Kane had Marion Davies closeted in the castle in *Citizen Kane* (1941) or James Caan/Kathy Bates in *Misery* (1990)—that kind of crap. Control freak—I know the type. I grew up with them.

At the time I swear to God I never knew what Izzy Clurman was capable of. It was only later all those women came forward to tell how they'd been grabbed, poked, raped, assaulted. Freaks. Sex freaks. Pussy-grabbers. Dick exhibitionists. Hollywood's full of them. Worse than Washington.

But as disgusting as Clurman and Rayna were, I had to admit: they could sure put on a show.

One of the abiding characteristics of a big mansion—and this is true of your midcentury modern, Tudor, classic revival—I don't care what form your architectural monstrosity takes—there's always a lot of leafy grounds and big windows to visually partake of those grounds, and it doesn't take a genius to figure out if you can see out, some voyeuristic weirdo like me (okay, I confess—sue me) is going to have the capability to hang around outside behind a tree, up a tree, or a hundred other spots, and watch you and all the funk you do.

Izzy Clurman and Rayna Rourke did it all.

Trust me, wish I'd had a camera. With a telephoto lens. If Rayna makes it big, I could rake in a fortune.

You might wonder what I thought of what went on between Izzy and Rayna on a personal, non-commercial level. I honestly don't know. It disturbed me, but not in any jealous way. It turned me on, I have to admit that. Though he kept in shape, Clurman wasn't much to look at; Rayna was another story. Men would have died to have what Clurman had at that moment in time. Was he grateful? Not a bit. He mistreated her mercilessly. You could see the cruelty from way far across the property line, even without the binoculars.

I turned away. I had something else to attend to that night.

I'd come across the name by mere happenstance, actually, and that's when the idea came to me.

His name was Porter and he lived in a nice little apartment building, a four-plex, southwest of Paramount off Melrose. Nice area, really, nestled away from the busy streets—Highland to the east, La Brea to the west. Hancock Park, I think, or nearby. The mayor lives around there. At night there isn't much foot-traffic, mostly dog-walkers. It's residential parking only but I wasn't going to be long; besides, it wasn't *my* car they'd be ticketing.

I found the address on the internet and got my phone-app to take me there. Now that I had finally arrived, the excitement tingled up my spine like a good horror movie just before one of those classic jump-scares you know is coming but there's nothing you can do about it short of storming the projection booth and ripping the hard-drive out of the projector.

There were tags on the doorbells, all in the same careful handwriting, a nice touch. My man Porter lived in the top right apartment. How to get in was the question of the evening. I tested the door to the small front foyer—locked. It would be easy enough to break the glass in the door, but whoever slapped the security-company sticker on had placed it right in the spot to warn me. I could ring and hope Porter would let me in via the intercom, but the chances of that were pretty far-fetched. I stepped to the side, off the porch, behind the bushes, ducking down below the front window of the ground-floor apartment. Voices could be heard from inside, an older man and woman, retired, deaf, but as loud as they talked to each other, I couldn't understand what they were saying over the blare of the TV, an old movie, Howard Hawks' *Monkey Business* (1952) (not the Marx Brothers film), written by Ben Hecht, one of my favorite writers. (He wrote Marilyn Monroe's *autobiography*—how Hollywood is *that!?*) *Monkey Business* (1952) stars Cary Grant, Ginger Rogers, Marilyn Monroe—you gotta see it. I know all the lines but this couple was ruining it with their constant squawking. I would've broken their window, climbed in and sliced both of them to death ala *Prowler* (1981) if it hadn't been for another one of those security stickers, (curiously) from an entirely different company, and for remembering my credo: E-O-T-P, "Eyes on the Prize," and that night the prize was Porter upstairs.

Footsteps interrupted my fevered musings. I shrunk even further down the wall to the ground, fingered my knife, and stared up at the porch. I was in the dark, but if one of them looked my way—

There were two of them, a man and woman, in their 30s—I had no idea if one of them was Porter—but neither looked down at me. They were engaged in chortling, trading humorous comments, getting the key in the lock, going in—

The door started to close behind them. I leapt forward, knife out, flicking it open with spring-loaded, lightning speed just like the product description on Amazon. I inserted the blade inside the jamb at the last possible second, and the door closed but did not lock on it. I fell back to my hiding place, listening to the man and woman. By the sound they hadn't climbed the stairs inside but instead were busy unlocking the other downstairs door to the apartment across from the older couple's.

I would wait until the arrivals were inside. I'd been smart and fast and discrete—qualities I'd perfected over the years. If I had jumped up on the porch, I would have been spotted. If I'd hesitated another second, the door would have locked me out. I'd been perfect, the way I like to be.

I waited another five minutes to be sure. Too much time and somebody could use that door again and shut it firmly, or worse, spot my switchblade and confiscate it, or even call the cops— I hurried inside and up the stairs. For this next part, I had a plan, but there was no need for it; Porter's door was unlocked.

"Who's there?" he called, alarmed, jumping up from the living room couch, where he'd been watching an old rerun of *The Rockford Files* (1974-1980). I love *Rockford*. I was almost tempted to sit down and watch the episode with him—that would blow Porter's gourd—Angel Martin was just trying to cajole Rockford into aiding and abetting one of his creepy schemes—

"Who are you—" Porter stammered, the little creep.

I grabbed him and whirled him around, flicking the knife open, pressing it to his neck. He was smaller, older, skinnier, and less of a foe than I had imagined. I'd seen him in a few things. They must have been older pictures, or he just looked better altogether after hair and makeup.

"The question is," I hissed, breaking skin just a little, in case he didn't get the seriousness of the inquiry, "who are *you?*"

"P-P-P-Porter," he stuttered.

"Last name?" I wanted to know.

He gave it, and it was the right answer. I was in the right place. This was the right man and that was the right answer.

"Wrong answer!" I told him nevertheless, slicing the knife deeply across his throat, surprised at my own strength—I almost took his head off.

He gurgled and sputtered and fell to the floor, spraying, spewing, dumping buckets of blood and what smelled like urine on the faux-Persian rug—at least I thought it was *faux*. He was a working actor but hardly rich, evidenced by the contents of the apartment. His death had been so quiet, I took the opportunity to stay awhile and nose around among his things, maybe take a few items of value if they couldn't be traced. It was a smart move anyway, I figured—let the old folks downstairs go to sleep and the couple across the hall start their nightly "coupling"—I figured they would by the looks of them, grabby little bastards. Less chance of being spotted leaving.

Porter's life was a disappointment. His only interest was the movies, apparently, and he owned almost nothing of value, including his watch. Nevertheless, I took everything, along with his wallet ($37 and a couple credit cards), and put it all in a shopping bag. Sometime around midnight I left the apartment. I closed the door but didn't lock it. I wondered how long it would be until they discovered the body, so I went back and opened the door wide, exposing Porter covered in blood and piss on the floor, ensuring that the next person to come into that hall would see him.

Once out on the street, I walked past the car I'd driven up in. I left it parked and abandoned. It wasn't mine and I'd used gloves to drive it. In fact, I had gloves on all night—I wasn't worried. I left the shopping bag on a bus-bench on Melrose, including the $37 and the wallet, and started walking north and east, past Paramount and the other old studio lots, headed for the heart of Hollywood and my temporary home at the Arbuckle. With luck some poor loser would pick up Porter's things, pawn the watch and other valuables, use the credit cards, and get busted for Porter's murder.

That's how it went in *The Wrong Man* (1956) of course, and a thousand other hard-luck crime thrillers. You ever notice how they always play it from the innocent guy's point of view, never the winner of the deal, the one who gets away scot-free. I'd like to see that sometime. Why wallow in misery and injustice? Life's winners, those are the men we should be concerned about. A hundred people weep at some poor slob down on his luck on a movie screen but after the show's over and some dirty wino wants a little spare change for no other reason than he's asking, those same moviegoers pretend they don't see him or give him the evil eye or tell him to get a job like his dad owns the store or something and he can snap his fingers and go to work.

Don't get me started.

If you know Hollywood, you know the route I took: east on Melrose to Paramount, up Gower, past the Hollywood Forever Cemetery, once known as Hollywood Memorial Park. Gates close at 5 pm and it wouldn't have been a good idea to jump the wall this night, what with dead Porter still warm and just a few blocks behind me, but other nights I'd do it. Jayne Mansfield is in there, along with Rudolph Valentino, Douglas Fairbanks, Fatty Arbuckle, Bugsy Siegel, George Harrison, Judy Garland, Harry Cohn, Dee Dee Ramone, Johnny Ramone, Oleg Vidov (the Robert Redford of Russia), Clifton Webb—you name 'em, they're there. The place is known for its hauntings as well as its history of bankruptcy, mismanagement, criminal activity. A walk-through at night is not for the faint of heart.

I walked straight up Gower to the Sunset Gower Studios across from Gower Gulch, then took a right past the Sunset Bronson Studios. The studios' names change over the years—tell somebody these days, "The old Warner Hollywood Studios," they'll look at you like you're nuts or you belong back at Hollywood Memorial Park. It's all sound-stages for hire now anyway. The ownership doesn't matter anymore. It's a business like any other business.

That's me, T-C-O-B. Takin' Care of Business.

I made it home safely. Nobody had seen me, talked to me, taken any note of me whatsoever and I'd pulled my baseball cap (Boston, I don't know why—call it a tribute to Magnum) down low over my head and discarded it in the trash on the street. I walked with a limp just in case—"yeah, officer, I saw the guy—from Boston, walked with a limp."

While the funny gait seemed like a good idea at the outset, it was two miles northeast to my apartment. For the future, I tried to come up with something better—"he jogged with a limp, officer" didn't have the ring. Besides, guilty people run; innocent ones don't.

Finally, I neared my apartment building. A couple of cop cars sat in front, lights flashing. Not unusual at the Arbuckle, but it made my heart race and my head light from worry. I stayed far down the street in the shadows. A cap and limp weren't going to help me much if they'd already connected me somehow—wow, that was quick!—to a murder several miles away. If they were there for something else, they still might brace me and demand ID. I'd be in the system and in their memory, and if by some chance someone made the connection with me and Porter...

Also, I still had the knife. I loved that knife.

I waited. After a quarter of an hour, the four patrolmen ran from the building, jumped in their cars and took off, squealing their tires. Something had tossed them into action, perhaps the knifing death of an actor...

I took the long way around to the back door, pulling my collar high up over my face, walking confidently, a guy devoid entirely of limpitude. Security cameras were everywhere in the building but nobody watched them and it wasn't clear whether recordings were made. I was tired. I took the chance. I crawled into bed, worried, but still satisfied with the night's work. A job half-accomplished but well on its way to completion.

CHAPTER 12

Detective Larry Gregg couldn't believe how hard it was to find Lowanna Xanderson's talent agency. Everyone mistook him for a desperate actor. He looked it, actually, with a chiseled chin, a good voice, and he seemed like a guy who could carry a gun. He'd be a bit player of course. The Minnesota accent had to go—people told him that. But they claimed to have no idea how to get hold of Julie Baker's agent, Lowanna Xanderson. Her phone number, her address, even her location every minute of every day was a deeply held secret that Hollywood kept for her. It was a testament to how important she was that nobody could find her, not even a trained detective like Larry Gregg. Finally, Gregg called back to Rayna's roommate, who had no idea either. There was no phone number in the apartment from what Miss Arento could tell, and Gregg's search of Julie's room had yielded nothing.

"I wouldn't mind having that number myself," the roommate chuckled on the phone.

By all rights, Lowanna Xanderson's contact information would be in Rayna's phone, but Gregg had no idea Rayna's phone was probably down the gutter on Sunset, something George Landon had figured out, but which Gregg had yet to uncover in his notes. Finally Larry Gregg called Freddy Weaver, the acting coach, again. Freddy had mentioned Lowanna Xanderson, just like the roommate.

"You know how to find her?" Gregg asked him on the phone.

Freddy laughed.

"Is there some *other* way to find her?" Gregg tried again.

Freddy laughed even louder.

"Even if I knew, I wouldn't tell you," Freddy told Gregg from the safety of distance. "Lowanna Xanderson is a powerful person in this town. She'd have my hide. I need that connection even though I've never actually met her. Someday I will use that 'in'—trust me."

"You're kidding."

"One can only hope, right?"

"Seriously, I just want to ask her some questions," Gregg tried again, getting angry.

"Good-bye. Have a nice day," Freddy replied on his way to hitting "End" on his phone.

Larry Gregg felt like he'd wandered down a rabbit hole like Joseph Cotton in *The Third Man* (1949). The only thing missing was the zither.

He called the Screen Actors Guild, known simply as "SAG" in the biz.

They laughed at him and told him to forget it—"We don't give out that kind of information."

Larry Gregg wondered how anybody ever made a movie in Hollywood. How did producers get actors? How did actors get parts? If you couldn't find the agents...? It was all designed to keep people *out*, and detective Larry Gregg was as far out as you could possibly be.

He phoned information to see if there was a listing for Lowanna Xanderson. There wasn't. He tried the internet—same there, just a thousand photographs. Gregg thought: it's like the agent doesn't exist except to be photographed at film premieres with various clients—household names, stars Larry Gregg could only dream of meeting. Beautiful women, handsome men, great actors. Directors and producers were all represented by Lowanna Xanderson as well, but how to get their names, how to get their phone numbers, and how to get to her—

Gregg sat in his car outside Tommy's Famous Burgers, one of twenty "original locations," and wondered in frustration what was so famous about these hamburgers, and how to find Lowanna Xanderson. He supposed he could wait till nightfall and look for a premiere—

Gregg called information again.

"Let's see," the operator told him, trying to be helpful, "licensed talent agents...she's probably got an unlisted number..."

"Ya think?" Gregg asked sarcastically, taking it out on the poor operator— "Wait, wait—did you say 'licensed?'"

"Yes."

"So look that up," Gregg insisted, excited. "The licensing bureau. There must be a licensing department. In Fresno? That's the capital of California, right?"

Gregg searched back into his grade school education—

"I don't know," the operator laughed. "I'm not in California. I'm in Mumbai."

"Mumbai?"

"Yes. India."

"Thank you very much. Have a nice day," Gregg ended the call quickly.

The detective googled Fresno and to his surprise, it wasn't the capital at all. But he was soon clued to Sacramento. Another surprise: he got the "talent agency license database," which he searched. *Who knew such a thing existed?* Gregg marveled. There it was, right on the internet: Lowanna Xanderson's address.

Larry Gregg shook his head with a tiniest bit of regret. He'd already been scheming to call the California State Film Commission, pretending to be a big-shot producer making a film called...he tried to come up with something right away off the top of his head but it was useless—all he came up with was *Argo* (2012), the fictional film used to extract US embassy workers from Iran in 1979.

The charade would have been fun, he thought, like something Rockford would do...

As he drove west through the heart of Hollywood, Gregg guessed that same disappointment was probably repeated thousands of times a day in "Tinsel Town"—imaginations fired up to play roles, build universes, construct worlds of make-believe, only to be shut down in the next minute when the industry moved on to something else, something shinier, like a toddler with Attention Deficit Disorder.

Lowanna Xanderson's building was a non-descript office complex across from the Beverly Center, right down from Cedar Sinai—parking $30 period, flat fee, no in-and-out—Larry Gregg would have to explain the extravagance to the Bakers back in the rust belt, who would no doubt consider it a scam, which it was.

Security was tight, but Gregg managed to slip by with some others entering the building.

"If you look like you belong, nobody bothers you," Gregg had learned long ago. In some situations that meant a suit and tie and briefcase; here it was a jogging suit, sunglasses, and a ring of keys ready to open an office door. Lowanna Xanderson's office was on the third floor, down at the end where a maintenance man wrestled with a hall window unlatched by those Santa Ana winds LA is known for.

"Hey, there, how's it going?" Gregg asked the man, who was too pre-occupied with his window to do more than nod.

Gregg found the door marked "International Talent Associates of Hollywood" or something equally as non-descript. Deciding not to knock, Gregg pushed right in.

The door flew open in a gust of wind and blew apart a stack of actors' pictures and résumés like a roadside bomb.

The receptionist—a cute young thing—squealed, jumped to her feet, teetered on ridiculously high heels, and tried to grab the glossies like a contestant on a 50s game-show in the "money tube."

"I'm sorry, I'm sorry," Gregg apologized, and wrangled as many of the pictures he could get hold of—smiling young faces mostly, some older, some intense, "smoldering"—

On the back of each photo was stapled a résumé— lists of shows the actor had done.

"Leave them alone," the receptionist ordered. "I got this. This happens all the time. Back away."

From somewhere she produced one of those huge janitor's brooms with a six-foot wide head, and began sweeping the 8x10s into a corner.

"I was just about to shred these anyway," the receptionist said. "Lowanna makes me shred 'em and put 'em in the recycling. Some of them put their Social Security numbers on there, the sweet, stupid idiots. So thanks for nothing and don't let the door hit you on the way out. Low doesn't see actors in the office, sorry."

"Low?"

"Lowanna, of course. Just go."

"I'm not an actor."

The receptionist stood tall and leaned her broom against the wall. She took a long, skeptical look at Larry Gregg.

"Okay, I like the detective outfit, but it's too 'on the nose,'" she told him. "You need to do one thing a little 'off'—"

"I'm not an actor," Gregg insisted.

"Don't lie, please. I hear lies all day—"

"I'm not. I'm not an actor. I *am* a private detective."

The receptionist laughed.

"Okay, you're 'method.' I get it." The receptionist took a seat behind the considerable piece of furniture separating her from whatever poor soul stood on the other side. She grabbed a bunch of actors' photos and started grinding away with the industrial-sized paper shredder on the floor at her side.

"I'm not lying. I really am a detective," Gregg repeated.

The receptionist took another look. She believed him, turning her nose up like an elephant had just filled the room with a giant elephant fart.

"I'm looking for an actress," Gregg pressed on loudly over the noise of the shredder, pulling out the picture of Julie Baker he'd been carrying next to his heart ever since Minnesota, "do you know this woman? Recognize her?"

The receptionist shook her head before she really looked at the picture, then moved her eyes away. Gregg moved the photo, gently forcing her to look for real.

"Her name's Julie Baker or Rayna Rourke," he said. "She's a client of Ms. Xanderson. One of her actresses."

The receptionist scrunched her eyes in consternation and looked again at the photograph.

"No, she's not," the young go-getter was certain. "I would have known about her. She'd be in our files. I'd have spoken to her on the phone, had her sign papers."

"Maybe it hadn't gotten to that point yet," Gregg suggested.

The young woman looked up, something about registering. Maybe the receptionist recognized the photo after all, or she herself was supposed to have been an actress. Perhaps "Low" had groomed her the same way she was grooming Rayna there. There was some mystery involved—Gregg sensed it and his cop's nose had never let him down.

"Something you want to tell me?" Gregg asked softly, encouraging intimacy. "I'd really like to find this girl. She might be in trouble."

"That's..." the receptionist started to say, almost a gasp. She put her hand to her face like she was going to scream. Tears came to her eyes.

"What is it?" Gregg asked, summoning his kindest, most empathetic voice.

"Nothing," the young woman said. "Nothing. I'll write out a memo about your visit and email it to Lowanna. If she knows anything, she'll call you."

"Isn't she inside that door?" Gregg pressed, pointing to a closed, unmarked inner office door.

"I can't tell you that."

Gregg considered barging in. If the door was locked, would he give up then? How embarrassing would that be? How fast would the cops get there if he did? Would he be on the cover of *Variety* and *The Hollywood Reporter* and *The LA Times*?

"Will you show her the picture?" Gregg asked plaintively, fantasy over.

"I'll show it to her."

Gregg put it on the desk, away from the ones being shredded—

"Keep it. I have copies."

Gregg stopped leaning against the upright partition and stood tall. The receptionist knew something, he was sure, but Gregg also knew now wasn't the time to ask. Whatever she was hiding, she intended to keep it secret, at least for now. Gregg's job would be to figure out enough of it to force the rest out of her the next time they met. He was like a lawyer in this, believing he shouldn't ask a question of a witness unless he himself already knew the answer.

"So how do they know where to send you pictures?" Larry Gregg asked, pointing to the actors' photos, pocketing an agency business card with the other hand, "I had a hell of a time getting your address."

The receptionist shrugged.

"No idea, but they do. Somehow they do. She's dead, isn't she?" the receptionist asked, tapping on Julie Baker's photograph.

"Why do you say that?" Gregg wanted to know.

"Go. Go. Just go," the receptionist told him. She looked like she was going to cry. "And on the way out—"

"I got it," Gregg answered, holding the door open just a sliver, slipping out, keeping those Devil Winds at bay.

CHAPTER 13

I read the news today—oh boy. The papers and the broadcasts were all full of the dead actor in Hancock Park—his gruesome murder, the head almost severed from the body. Robbery was considered the motive. The old man and the old woman in the apartment below were interviewed—nothing original there:

"Who would ever think something like this would happen *here*?"

"We didn't hear a thing."

"I guess no place is safe anymore, is it?"

I watched in fascination and glee. They made a big deal out of how close it was to the mayor's house, like that had anything to do with it at all. I laughed.

It was just a matter of time now. I would wait. Maybe tomorrow I'd make that call. I didn't want to wait too long. It was like that knife in the door thing—too soon and somebody would notice. Too late and that would be it—too late—I'd lose my chance.

The excitement was too much to bear. I need to do something to occupy myself. I decided to go to the big-box home-improvement store and buy a couple of 30-pound bags of lime, the kind they use on lawns. I thought I'd roll them back to the apartment building in a shopping cart—I'd left the car, remember? I had yet to pick up another one. No need, not yet. But then I got stuck on how much lime to get. Maybe one shopping cart wasn't enough. If the movies were correct, this would dissolve the evidence. But when I googled "how much lime to dissolve bones?" according to strangers on the internet that was all bunk and lime actually *preserves* human remains. Acid is what I needed, hydrochloric to be exact, like Jeffrey Dahmer used. Guess what? Not readily available. What I could get was muriatic acid, for swimming pools, or sulfuric acid for cleaning out drains. Price and quantity was an issue—I might not be able to buy out the store's supply of drain cleaner without attracting suspicion (acid can be used for explosives, too, apparently—red flag on *that*).

Residents gathered at the front of the building. Agitated, they whispered in frightened tones of the return of Mavis Banning, the ghost in the water tower, who had apparently returned that night, the reason for the cops' appearance. Several of the residents had seen her walking the halls threatening revenge. I paused and listened—not that I believed any of those loonies, many of whom were certified nut-jobs who could show you the paperwork on it—state and federal. But it couldn't hurt to listen in, seeing as Elena Mejia's bones were still up there now, and I might need to stay ahead of that curve. I also...well, this is hard to admit...I'd seen things in the building, heard things, felt things, that I couldn't exactly explain. I have two feet firmly on the ground, believe me, and I don't for a minute believe in ghosts, but I'd be a fool not be open to the idea of another world, another dimension, a place where people go when they're dead, a drop of the supernatural plopping into our daily life-puddles on occasion.

So I went with four two-gallon boxes of muriatic acid, which, if you do the math and "a pint's a pound the world around" still, that's sixty-four pounds of liquid I hauled home.

Emboldened by all my recent successes, I ran the acid right up to the top floor in the elevator, then carried it up to the roof via the stairs. Nobody saw me; I was living right. Even carrying the gallon jugs up the ladder wasn't a big deal. Call it adrenaline; I felt like Superman that morning. I dumped the acid all over Elena Mejia's bones, all eight gallons. In the large tank, it didn't cover her much, but it was a start. This was an experiment, after all.

I'd dumped the bones out of the compostable plastic bags, in case you're wondering—I needed to see the bones themselves dissolve in full view.

Leonarda Cianciulla. If there's one cannibal and axe murderer you should know about, that's her. She lived in Correggio, Italy, in the 1930s and killed her best friend (*three* best friends, actually) as some sort of human sacrifice to the gods. Leonarda lured her victims via postcards and letters the same way creepos lure their victims today except now they do it with the internet and emails and text-messages.

"Don't tell anyone about this," Leonarda always told them. She killed three women, at least that's all anyone knows about, who she catfished to town on the promise of a job or a husband. She chopped them up into large pieces and boiled them in a giant cauldron. She turned them into soap. That's right, *soap*, not soup. (Well, soup too.) Ingenuous. Wish I'd thought of it. Took their money as well. She gave the bars of soap away as presents to friends and family on special occasions and holidays. Again, a nice touch. Not that soap isn't fairly inexpensive at the local store, and besides, who has the time for homemade soap anymore? Still, you have to admire the pluck.

Ever buy soap on Etsy? Well, think again.

What Leonarda didn't make into soap, she turned into tea-cakes using her victim's blood. Pretty basic recipe apparently, with chocolate. The secret ingredient? Love.

I can't believe nobody has made a full-length feature film about Leonarda Cianciulla. Somebody should. I ought to write it. How hard could that be? Except I'd change it to the U.S. What do I know about Italy a hundred years ago? Besides, people enjoy American movies. They like the fresh-faced optimism and the up-from-nowhere, rah-rah enthusiasm, even while scores of actors are getting mowed down by Uzi fire or blasted to little bits by explosives hurled from the cold, dead hands of interplanetary robots. Rayna could be in it. She'd be Leonarda with an axe. The thing writes itself.

When I got back down to my apartment the noon news was all about Porter again. By then they'd gotten hold of his movie clips and were airing scenes. The mayor had yet to comment, even though he lived only a few blocks away.

I couldn't stand it. I'd take the chance. This was big news now and I did *not* want to miss my chance. I pulled out my phone.

"Screen Actors Guild," some plebe at the union answered.

"Yeah, I need to talk to somebody about my membership—"

The twerp didn't even bother to answer, just clicked to another department. I listened to light jazz.

"Membership," another rude functionary answered.

"Yes," I began, "I am a member of the guild and I need to talk to somebody about my membership—"

"Specifically, what?"

"I need to get my real name back."

"Okay...? I don't get it."

"When I joined the Screen Actors Guild," I explained patiently, "I was forced to choose a different name than my own—"

"'Cause somebody was using it—happens all the time. I get it now," the official interrupted, eager to get on with his life, like I was some sort of annoyance. I could get his name and deal with him later the way I'd dealt with Porter, but I reminded myself I needed to keep my EOTP (Eyes On The Prize), and TCOB (Take Care of Business). After all, IPTBC (It Pays To Be Cautious).

"But now I'd like to reclaim my name," I said.

"You can't—not if somebody else is using it."

"But they're not," I argued.

"What's the name? I'll look it up."

"Porter Skully," I replied.

There was a long pause at the other end of the line.

"Porter Skully," the man said, dripping sarcasm. It wasn't a question but I answered it anyway:

"Yes, Porter Skully."

"What are you trying to pull here, bro? What is this, some kind of sick joke?" he asked in a low, confidential voice, the kind you'd use on a crazy person.

"It's not a joke. I'm Porter Skully—"

"You're *not* Porter Skully. Porter Skully is dead." I could hear him getting angry now. "He was murdered. Last night in his apartment—I got the TV on right here—the mayor's going to speak in a minute—"

"I'm the real Porter Skully—"

"So this dead guy—he's a figment of somebody's imagination?"

"I mean I'm the *original* Porter Skully. Porter Skully is my real name and I want to get it back."

"Well, you can't—"

"I can show you my birth certificate," I told him, then remembered: "Actually, I just ordered it from the State of Oregon—"

"Doesn't matter."

"What do you mean it doesn't matter?"

"It doesn't matter 'cause the guy registered the name first and it's his forever—"

"But he's *dead*."

"*Forever's* longer than dead, *bro*. Besides, his films live on, his *credits* live on. You don't want to be claiming credit for work he did, do you?"

I thought about that. It wasn't a bad idea. Porter Skully had a pretty decent career. They were showing the clips. I could just pick up where he left off. I would already have a long list of credits on IMDB. Problem was I didn't look a bit like the actor I killed, and the way he died caused a small sensation, so now people connected the name with the face—

I had to admit, I might have screwed up royally. A quiet death might not even have made the news. With a quiet death they might have even given me his name without a fuss. After all, he was only a bit player...*who I made a star!*

"Hello, you there?" the SAG man asked on the phone.

I wasn't sure what to say.

"I think we're done here," he concluded. "Have a nice day."

The guy hung up on me.

CHAPTER 14

"When a man's partner is killed, he's supposed to do something about it," Sam Spade was telling Brigid O'Shaughnessy on the TV in Larry Gregg's motel room. "It doesn't make any difference what you thought of him." Gregg turned down the sound and lip-synched the next line in his best Bogart: "He was your partner and you're supposed to do something about it."

Larry Gregg shut off the TV. He'd seen *The Maltese Falcon* (1941) a hundred times. He'd even read the book, and he'd read fewer than a dozen works of fiction in his entire life. The uncanny irony that he was now living the movie, more or less, was not lost on him. The coincidence of the film coming on at 8 am in his motel room while on the case, instantaneous, without him looking for it—eerie, weird, totally off the charts.

The city was haunted, Gregg truly believed at that moment, and he hadn't believed in anything like that his entire life, not since the tooth fairy.

He shivered, put on his jacket—LA was cold this time of year, no matter what people in Minnesota might think.

"I usually spend my break walking," Clyde Grogan told Larry Gregg.

"Sure," Gregg said. "Let's walk."

They went south and west at a brisk pace. It was all Gregg could do to keep up with the younger man.

"Yeah, I have no idea what happened to Rayna," Clyde said right out. "She just stopped coming to class. That's not that unusual, to tell the truth. If an actor gets a job, even a civilian job—they might have to drop out.

That's why Freddy makes you pay in advance. Also, actors don't have much money sometimes."

"It's tough, I imagine," Gregg said.

"So maybe Rayna just got a waitress gig or something," Clyde offered.

"Not according to her roommate," Gregg stated.

"How about home? She didn't go home?"

"Not to the Midwest. Her parents are very worried," Gregg told the struggling actor.

"That other guy...the other detective?" Clyde asked.

"George Landon. I'm looking for him, too. He was a friend of mine."

Clyde Grogan stopped cold. He surveyed the area, a poorer section of Hollywood, tenement apartments, on-street parking, women and children this time of day and guys working on their cars, 90% Hispanic, though there were others from all over the world.

"That's rough," he said. "This is where I usually head back."

But he made no move to walk in that direction, nor did he look Gregg in the eye, either.

"They both just fell into a black hole, it seems..." Gregg spoke softly.

"I have an idea," Clyde told the detective in a voice so small Gregg could barely make it out over the late-morning traffic. "There's a guy in acting class...'Jack C. Cunningham' but that's not his real name, I don't think. Hell, none of us use our real names. He's a total bull-shitter. I mean, everybody's a bull-shitter here, but he..."

Clyde didn't look like he was going to continue. Gregg recognized the name "Jack C. Cunningham" from George Landon's notes.

"What makes you think this Cunningham—"

"Nothing. Nothing specific," Clyde spat out angrily. "I got nothing. Just a darned feeling up my spine and into my brain. He knew Rayna. He was after her like a hawk goes for a prairie dog—crush her under a million tons of pressure in its talons—"

"Did he ever do anything, say anything...?"

Clyde was already shaking his head.

"If I were you, I'd go after him," was all he said, "and I'd do it at an angle. I don't mean to tell you your business, but your friend showed too many cards too early I'll bet, and got cut out of the game before the bets were in."

Detective Gregg stared at the young man. Clyde didn't seem like much of a poker player—

"I gotta run now," the young man said, taking off, hurrying back to the grocery store where he worked.

Gregg let him go.

CHAPTER 15

The one thing the Skullys taught me was how to live off the land. It didn't matter if that land was out in the woods or in a densely populated urban setting like Hollywood, the principles are the same. I was abandoned, forced to live in the compound in Oregon, never to see my real mother and father again. So I adapted to the Skully's weird habits and ideas. They ate meat. Protein was sacred. They don't grow vegetables but they pick vegetables and berries and anything hanging from a tree. Nuts. They live off the land. They put up hundreds of no trespassing signs to scare everyone away. But then, sometimes when they get hungry enough...they take the signs down...

It's all protein; that's what I learned. Blame them.

When it came time for me to go to school, Rose took me into town in the pickup and I met the principal and there were a lot of forms to fill out, which we took home. Rose and Mack argued about it. I don't remember who argued what or who won, but it was decided I would be home-schooled like all my brothers and sisters, which meant we'd learn to read and write and the basics of arithmetic, but almost nothing about the outside world except "it's all shit, that's what it is."

All of us children all had chores, morning till night. There was a great deal of cleaning up even though you couldn't really say anything was clean. We had a bath once a week in the creek, no matter how cold it was or what time of the year. In the summer it was refreshing; in the winter it would turn your lips blue and you had pains in your chest and you thought you were going to die.

We were taught "don't talk about the family or where you live or what it's like or how many times you get beaten every day." Nobody went in or out of the compound without permission, under threat of severe punishment. Mack and Rose instilled in us a profound fear of punishment, which we knew we deserved because they also taught us that there were horrible things wrong with us.

"And don't forget you're a liar," Rose told me a hundred times, "and nobody's ever going to believe you anyway since you're a kid and a known liar."

The "Butcher Barn" was profoundly off-limits. Going in there or even peeking inside could get you a beating, but then you could be beaten at any moment—anywhere, anytime—in your clothing or stripped naked for all the world to see, no reason need be given.

"Life's not fair, we are not fair, you're a worthless piece of shit!" Rose or Mack or one of the older kids would yell at you while they whacked you with something they'd just grabbed for the purpose. "Forget fair! You are here to serve the *community*, not yourself!"

But to top it all off...the greatest indignity...which faced me right smack in the face when I opened the mail eagerly...was that the State of Oregon was in cahoots with the whole evil conspiracy. I was right there buried deep inside a Bourne movie. I had no idea who I was, because I held in my hand:

STANDARD CERTIFICATE OF LIVE BIRTH, STATE OF OREGON, BOARD OF HEALTH—PORTLAND, FEDERAL SECURITY AGENCY—U.S. PUBLIC HEALTH SERVICE. CHILD'S NAME: Porter Haynes Skully. FATHER'S NAME: Jackson McDonald Skully. MOTHER'S NAME: Rosemary Ann Skully (nee Ingersoll).

What a joke. A scam, as sophisticated as *The Usual Suspects* (1995), as goofy as *Paper Moon* (1973). I was adopted and given to the Skullys. No possibility I was born to Rose and Mack in— I looked for the hospital name: "St. Mary's in Portland." What a sham! Made-up, phony, fake news, clear as Julie Christie's eyes in *Doctor Zhivago* (1965), and twice as dangerous.

This thing went deep—that was obvious. To ferret out the culprits and bring them to justice would take all my resources and ingenuity. I needed to stay sharp, build myself up—like that sequence in every Rocky movie, and all the other movies, too. I'd have to drag a locomotive by my teeth or carry great bags of fertilizer up stadium steps, a thousand push-ups, a thousand sit-ups—

Who was I kidding? My brain was my muscle. It was all I needed.

And a car.

I checked my watch. Enough time to steal one and bring it home. Nobody walks in LA. Only losers take the bus.

By the time I got it home—silver Japanese car—and changed the license plates—from a silver-beige Chrysler—and taped over the visible VIN number on the dash—it was time to go to Freddy Weaver's class. Even though Rayna had stopped coming, and I was damned certain Freddy could teach me absolutely nothing about acting or show-business I didn't already know, I went to class anyway. Someone might notice if I missed it—that cop, for instance, the one who'd been there on Tuesday night, pretending to be an agent or a manager or a producer of some kind.

P-I-C—that's my motto. Play it Cool. Don't try anything out of the ordinary. Don't make any sudden, unexpected moves. Sure, I was upset, devastated, angry beyond all reason—Charles Foster Kane-angry from *Citizen Kane* (1941), Robin Williams-angry in *The Angriest Man in Brooklyn*, Joe Pesci-angry in every movie he's ever been in.

I checked the computer. People "like me, hundreds, with new "likes" every day, on all sorts of platforms. I had the pick of any woman I wanted, though the percentage who lived within reasonable driving distance was quite small. I don't get internet sex at all. I like the real thing. Touching, feeling, juices, blood. Somebody to join poor, lonely Helen Majors up in the tank and in the various bins around the apartment.

The girls on the net seemed eager and easy enough. There were the usual obvious hustlers, and some not-so-obvious, and some honeys, but it all just made me more hungry than horny.

I threw a steak on a frying pan on the stove. A little garlic, pepper—I don't like to get too fancy, and I like it reasonably well-done—we're not animals here, and this meat wasn't exactly USDA inspected. By the time I'd eaten my steak, salad on the side, plus some Sara Lee apple pie for dessert, the urge to murder and mayhem was over. I pulled myself together.

"Sorry, not tonight, ladies," I told those bitches on the 'net, turning off the computer. "Other fish to fry." I grabbed my keys and started walking.

CHAPTER 16

Detective Larry Gregg waited in his car just down the street from the acting studio. It had taken him hours for a good spot to open up where he could watch the door in his car instead of standing, fiddling with his phone, pretending to be waiting for someone, not unlike the many hookers—male and female—who populated this section of Sunset, plying *their* trade. It was obvious to them Gregg was no competition, and was probably, in fact, heat.

Gregg ticked off the students entering the acting school. George Landon had worked up a complete list. Gregg spotted Clyde going in, then Jack C. Cunningham, the object of Gregg's interest this night.

Gregg took out George Landon's case-book and went through it one more time. He paused on the name "Jack C. Cunningham." There was an address as well. If Gregg was going to follow Cunningham after class, he figured, it might help to know where he was headed.

Gregg googled the address, hoping for a map. He'd see if it was within walking distance, *or had Jack driven?* Gregg hadn't seen a car pull up, but then the parking was scarce here—none of the actors seemed to have a car.

As soon as Gregg entered Jack's address, the detective's phone came alive with newspaper articles on the hotel where Jack lived. The building was famous, apparently, *infamous* actually.

Mavis Banning, the articles said, also known by her porn-star name, Mindy Minx, had died there. An engineering student from Finland, she'd stayed to work in an aerospace facility in the Seattle-Tacoma area before moving to Los Angeles to pursue a career in acting. Some said she'd been let go up north because of a slow-down in the industry, others claimed she had visa difficulties, others blamed the president's crackdown on immigration. There were whispers of affairs with other employees. All agreed Mavis Banning was a "stone-cold knockout."

She had many friends and relatives, both in Seattle and back in Finland, and picked up even more friends in a year or two in Los Angeles, so when she went missing—this was ten years ago, Larry Gregg noted—her disappearance was widely reported and noted, and an investigation was opened.

The fact she had by then embarked on a career path in the sex-film business was not lost on the authorities. To their surprise, the single homicide did not turn into a serial killer situation as far as they could tell. No other porn-stars were killed; there were no notes in blood explaining the motive—no "Die, you worthless harlot!" messages—and the police weren't mocked, taunted, or otherwise bothered. No cat and mouse whatsoever.

"The thing writes itself," the Assistant Police Chief told the press, "but nobody bothered."

What was striking, and unusual, was the discovery of Mavis's body in the water tank on the roof of the hotel where Jack C. Cunningham now lived ten years later. It was the kind of thing George Landon reveled in.

"There are no coincidences!" Landon would say. His pal Larry Gregg always took the other side, arguing that chance, happenstance, randomness, "the luck of the draw," was as important as logic sometimes, especially when it came to solving a case.

Mavis Benning was said to be a porn "star," but what Larry Gregg was reading on the internet indicated the "star" was just a convention.

"They're all 'stars,'" he muttered to himself.

The newspaper articles described her eventual addiction to drugs—crack cocaine mostly—and her descent into prostitution to pay for the habit. She had set up a rather lucrative business connected to the smut whereby someone watching a film could then get in touch with her personally and recreate the same scene in person, in real life, in actual time.

"George would have looked into that, definitely," Larry Gregg told himself aloud in the car, looking up through the windshield, checking the door to the acting studio again. Nothing stirring. Gregg looked at his watch. Another half-hour to go. He went back to Mavis.

There were still two other angles to exploit when it came to the dead woman: the supernatural one, and the mental illness aspect. Both presented bizarre possibilities. Surveillance cameras in the building showed Mavis acting strangely, hurrying in and out of elevators, running up and down stairs, through hallways, into and out of rooms, *right through walls!*

Gregg recognized the ghostly effect from various *Paranormal* movies.

Opinions varied on the strange behavior: mental illness, demon possession, a general haunting. Nobody said CGI. The manager of the building explained that the shadowy jerkiness was merely a defect of the surveillance cameras and the recording equipment, "long-since replaced," he assured everyone.

Gregg watched the various angles again. Mavis seemed to be speaking throughout, though there was no sound. Her lips moved quickly, animated, pixelated. She wore a glitter-covered hooded sweatshirt, zipped low, emphasizing her pronounced breasts. Her jeans, two sizes too small, were bedazzled with some sort of shiny material. High heels completed the outfit. She walked forward, then back, head moving side to side and back and forth, as if stretching. Her eyes flew wildly from one side to the next. Her hands and arms were busy, too, flailing, twisting, not quite dancing but a possible parody of some Asian exercise routine. She could have been on drugs—

She's running, Gregg decided. *Somebody's after her and she doesn't know which way to go. She's scared shitless, too. She can barely contain herself. She can't control her muscles, she's so scared.*

Gregg shivered involuntarily. The car was cold now, with sundown hours before. Gregg ducked down behind the dashboard—the actors were just coming out of the studio. Some spoke to each other, cigarettes were lit, but the object of Gregg's interest that night did none of those things. Jack C. Cunningham moved down the other side of the street, past Gregg, headed east. Gregg checked his rear-view mirror. When the coast was clear, he slipped out of the car and followed on foot, careful not to be seen. Gregg had never been much good at a tail—he'd just been unlucky, he supposed, or was never really trained—

Sure enough, Jack turned a corner. By the time Gregg hustled down to the end of the block—Hollywood Boulevard—Jack was running full out through casual strollers, costumed superheroes, movie-goers, drunks and hookers.

Damn, Gregg told himself. He took a breath. It didn't matter. He knew where Jack lived. Gregg took his time getting there.

There was no sign of Jack outside the apartment building. Gregg waited a few minutes to consider his next move. Distracted and disturbed by a transvestite jerking off a customer in plain sight in the alley, Gregg moved once again, only to be confronted by a disembodied face sticking out from a mountain of blankets, demanding money in a strange language Gregg didn't recognize. The detective hoped there was a body under there sitting on the sidewalk. He fished in his pocket, pulled out some change and dropped it into the toothless man's (woman's?) bloated, black hand.

A pirate—tri-cornered hat, peg leg, eye patch, bottle of rum—wandered past brandishing what looked like a real-life cutlass, sharp and deadly.

Gregg decided not to wait any longer. He went to try the door, looking up at the last moment, spotting the security cameras pointing back at him.

A young woman stormed out of the building just as Gregg arrived, swinging the door wide for Gregg to grab before it locked shut again.

"Thanks," he told her as he slipped inside the building.

The place was dark—that was Gregg's first impression. A single overhead bulb lit the front foyer, a worn, filthy remnant of the hotel's magnificent past, no doubt. Back in Mavis's day there had been many bulbs burning—incandescent bulbs with lots of watts, on a chandelier perhaps—not this single, curled-up worm of a 12-watt LED.

The detective allowed his eyes to adjust to the darkness for a minute, and he noted the tell-tale surveillance camera in the corner of the vaulted ceiling, its red lamp lit. Gregg wondered if it was for real, like its twin outside on the building monitoring the sidewalk, or if it was just some sort of dummy, going nowhere like the rest of Tinsel Town. The possibility someone was actually *monitoring* the camera never entered Gregg's mind, which quickly turned to figuring out the next move. Actually entering the building had been a sudden impulse; what to do now was a puzzle.

He remembered Clyde's admonition to come at Jack Cunningham at an angle, and he intended to do that, unlike with the other actors in Freddy's class who Gregg had questioned forthrightly.

Gregg suddenly had the urge to go up on the roof, check the water-tank, or tanks, see what was inside. Maybe George Landon's remains. Or something else.

That was crazy and Gregg knew it. That was George's "no coincidences" thinking. Just because there was once a dead body in the tub didn't mean there had to be another one. Just because Jack C. Cunningham lived here and just because he took an acting class with Julie Baker, who George had been looking for, and now he, Larry Gregg, was looking for in turn...

Gregg turned. He left the building and started the long trek back to his car. Whatever secrets the Arbuckle held, Gregg didn't want to know. Not that night.

CHAPTER 17

Call it guilt if you want. I don't feel it. Guilt's not in my playbook. I don't do guilt. The Skully's beat it out of me. It's true I hooked Rayna up with Izzy Clurman and he is a real piece of work. We were in competition on that, you could say, but I never stooped to some of the things I saw him do through those big-ass picture windows at night, every night. So maybe it *was* guilt. I felt sorry for Rayna, let's leave it at that.

Tonight's horror show was straight out of *A Clockwork Orange* (1971). Clurman had found some stud off the boulevard to do things in the rough with Rayna while Izzy watched for a while. Then he jumped into the fray and they tag-teamed her a bunch longer. She didn't have a chance.

Rayna started to blubber real tears and it was all I could do to maintain my observation post, but cooler heads prevailed (mine) and I let the scene play out in deference to the larger issues involved—Rayna's career, my career, our futures together. No matter what kind of bastard Izzy Clurman was, he could make or break someone in Hollywood, which is what we counted on most of all.

Rayna started screaming and to his credit, the big goof slacked off a little until Izzy yelled at him and then he started pumping again like the oil wells in *Giant* (1956). Izzy—the little shit—told Rayna to shut up and spanked her with a giant novelty paddle with holes drilled into it. I could hear the SLAP sound from way off.

It turned me on, I admit it, as it did the men in the room, I noticed, and I hoped Rayna enjoyed it just a little but I suspected she didn't. "If that's what it takes to make it in show business, that's what it takes," I wanted to tell her, soothe her frazzled nerves—

It was all I could take; I couldn't handle anymore. I climbed down from the tree I was in and high-tailed it across Izzy Clurman's yard to the lowest portion of the security wall. I climbed over and walked down into Hollywood. It's a nice view actually, the lights twinkling below. Everybody's got a dog, though, and they start yapping and barking and growling whenever anybody walks by, which kind of destroys the beauty of it. They bark on the way up, too, but eventually they shut up when I get situated in a tree or behind a bush to do the voyeur thing. I wonder if little Fluffy and big Fido mistake me for a bear or a mountain lion—both those things live up there—and figure they should shut up.

It's every creature for himself in the hills, believe me. I take care of myself, you know that. If you haven't learned anything else about me—

All that walking up and down the Hollywood Hills and west and south almost to Culver City keeps me in shape. I moisturize. I do my exercises. I eat meat almost exclusively and in moderation.

But I got stress. I have to admit it. It's killing me. Sometimes I have to let it out.

When I hit the boulevard, I heard music, disco, and I followed it. At night there's disco and rap and salsa music—you can get what you want. There's even country line-dancing probably if that's your thing. I didn't care. I wanted a drink, maybe two, and people—drunk people. Just to bring me out of my funk. Izzy and Rayna and that guy had done it to me and now I needed to wash that out with a strong astringent—Scotch or bourbon or gin.

The doorman was black, 35, 6 foot 9 and built like he'd spent the last five years pumping iron in state lockup. A couple of groups of young teens, about ten in all, hung around the door like they might have a chance of getting in, no matter they were nowhere near 21 years of age. The place was called "The Pit," which is what the sign said overhead—no other indication. Disco music came from inside, and some flashing lights, and the cover charge was only ten bucks, so I took a chance.

The guy looked me over pretty good and for a second I thought he was going to frisk me, which would've been iffy with the spring-loaded blade in my pocket, not that this guy looked like he'd call the police.

"Here's my sawbuck, sport," I told him, waving the bill in front of his face, distracting him like you would a stupid cat. When that didn't work, I gave him a look straight in the eyes that told him messing with me wouldn't come cheap. He let me by without a hassle, without laying a finger on me. Cops get that. Prison guys get that. I'm not somebody you want to bother.

The place was crowded, packed, with a home-made bar built on the other side. There were a few tables around the side and that was about it. Last week it might have been a comic-book store or a massage parlor or a manicure place—who can remember?

I pushed my way through the dancers, some of whom were very good, some terrible, and some just swaying to slosh the drugs around in their heads. I made it to the bar and took the last piece of leaning real estate available.

The talk around me was the usual bullshit: who's doing who, who's shooting a pilot, actors, acting class, rent, money, clothes, Final Draft or Movie Magic Screenwriter, Final Cut or Adobe Premiere. I ordered a double Scotch, put it down quickly, and signaled for another. When it didn't come fast enough I called the bartender lady—green hair, red lips, blue eyes—a fucking fauvist painting on LSD—a "fucking bitch" but with a smile on my face so I don't think she heard me, or maybe she just enjoyed that sort of abuse. With Rayna and Izzy doing their degradation thing every night, I was beginning to think I had it all wrong and people *like* the sort of blood-sport I grew up with. *Call it kink and let it go,* I told myself.

By then I'd had it up to here with the trio of actors next to me—two guys and a girl. They'd gone beyond whose agent said what to whom and what you needed to do to get into SAG anyway, and who was better "Stanislavski or Meisner?" to what was the best kind of waiter job to get so you could have your audition days free, and whether it was tacky to take Uber to a tryout. Would the casting people and director and producers notice or would they not, or even care that you didn't even have a fucking car?

"It's classy," one of the men said, "not to drive yourself."

I laughed out loud.

All three turned to me.

"Yeah, real classy—show up at Paramount in a ten-year-old Honda driven by a pimple-faced college student," I commented.

"Who the fuck are you?" the girl wanted to know. She had a mouth on her—

"Jack C. Cunningham—" I announced very distinctly. These ditzes were total assholes but then again, it didn't hurt to spread one's name around the acting community.

"And what the fuck do you know about it?" one of the guys asked, belligerent, not wanting the chick to out-cuss him.

"I'm an actor," I said cheerfully. When they go low, I go high. I heard that somewhere—

"An actor," the other guy repeated, thinking the same thing as me—*it wouldn't hurt to network a little even if the guy's a full-blown asshole.*

"Yeah, I'm studying with Freddy Weaver at the moment, his advanced technique class."

The girl was getting all pussy-wet, I could tell, impressed as all get-out. Maybe she'd tried out for Freddy Weaver's and hadn't made the grade or maybe she hadn't even gotten that far—it didn't matter, right then she was so hot for me she would've sucked it, humped it, stroked it or poked it—"choose your pleasure, lad!"

"Freddy Weaver sucks," the first of the male actors commented, kind of ruining the moment for me and my new acquaintance.

"What did you say?" I challenged, catching my breath.

"You heard me," he said. "Freddy Weaver sucks. He's a sexual predator, a dirty old man, an exhibitionist and a pedophile."

"A pedophile?" I scoffed. Okay, maybe some of his actresses were technically underage—

"You heard me," the man said, his "go-to" line. "So how'd you get in his class? Suck his dick or did he fuck you in the ass?"

That did it. A guy's supposed to stick up for his teacher, his *sensei*, his mentor, but frankly it was the fag-talk that put me over the edge.

Somebody jostled me in the back on the other side and I used that as an excuse to let go of my drink and drop to the floor—"excuse me"—and once on the floor I flicked my knife open and stabbed it through this fucking jerk-off's orange and green custom-made Nikes just far enough so you could hear his scream slightly over the disco but not so much it nailed his little piggies to the wood floor. I pulled the knife back out, clicked it shut and crawled my way down a couple thicknesses of semi-conscious dancing couples before getting back on my feet and pushing further through the maelstrom. I'd lost my bearings by that time, but then I spotted the men's room and decided to go for it. If there was a window, I could get out that way and not pass the doorman in case he was good at describing people to police or maybe he was studying to be a police sketch-artist himself, who knew? Anything's possible. To say I wasn't thinking quite straight at that moment would be an understatement. I'm pretty sure it was the Scotch.

The men's room was a zoo full of homosexuals doing things to each other I won't bore you with, but there were a couple of guys at one of the sinks putting together lines of cocaine which did interest me. I figured I needed the energy to crawl out the high window that presented itself to me on the back wall. So I shoved the first guy aside—

"Hey!"

—and stabbed him in the neck.

"Jesus!" was all his buddy could say as I stepped between them both, pushing them back, taking the coke myself, both full lines, right and left nostril, blocking the fountain of blood with my hand that shot out from the first guy's neck, keeping it from contaminating the cocaine—

The men's room cleared out pretty quickly. Sex or no sex, everybody wanted to get as far from the blood as possible, so it was now only me and the now-dead man on the floor. I checked his pockets and came up with a wallet and more of the drugs, and keys. I took all of it.

I climbed on the last sink near the window and managed to crawl out. It was only a six-foot drop to the alley below—no sweat. Once on the street, I circled the block looking for the guy's car, pushing the unlock button every ten feet or so. There was an alarm on the fob, too, but I didn't push it—with my luck the alarm would go off next to the last man on Earth who would take an interest in it...or a cop.

Finally, I got a hit on a twenty-year-old Nissan. I jumped in behind the wheel and that's when all hell broke loose with a big guy coming in the passenger's side and another one jumping in the back behind me and wrapping his big-ape arm around my neck, pressing me back against the headrest, choking me out. My hand was in my pants in a second for the knife but so was the guy in the front seat—

"What's this? What's this?" he exclaimed, amused by my blade, which he flicked open a couple times like a kid at Christmas.

"I can't breathe," I protested, and they both laughed.

"Take the car," I choked. "Just take it."

They both laughed again.

"Who wants this piece of shit?" the one in the front asked, I think, though I was struggling to maintain consciousness and not all my brain-cells were working. "You got any credit cards?"

"No, take the car," I repeated.

They rifled through my pockets, and quickly hit pay-dirt.

"Lookie here! Lookie lookie lookie!" they shouted out, taking all my money, which was considerable, most of the thirty-five thousand Jaime had given me, in cash, stuffed in my pockets, shoes, socks, underwear. The little fucks found it all plus the drugs, and didn't give a damn what they touched or destroyed doing it. Both of them hooted like pirates all the while and there was nothing I could do but try to keep breathing and hope they didn't stab me with my own switchblade.

Then they were gone as quickly as they had come. I was devastated but still alive, and it took all my strength not to scream bloody midnight murder on the streets of Hollywood in a piece of shit Nissan car I did not own.

L-O-T-F-A-D, I told myself—"Live On To Fight Another Day." I was also D-G-I-F-ing the hell out it as well as pausing, exhaling and acknowledging "to beat the band," as my stepfather Mack would say.

The loss of the money was a big blow but I told myself people have big blows happen to them all the time—floods, fires, earthquakes, hurricanes, tornadoes—and L-O-T-F-A-D like crazy. What with climate change, who knew what disaster would be next? How did people cope with such tremendous loss?

I don't care. I care about myself. That's who I care about and the only person I'm *supposed* to care about. Anybody tells you otherwise is a liar or bucking for some of that sweet Nobel Prize money.

I had to laugh. The crooks left my switchblade. It sat open on the ratty passenger's seat of the Nissan. They could have stabbed me, put an end to it, made sure I didn't identify them down the line. It would have been easy. Fools.

I picked up the knife, stuck it in my pocket, pulled my pants up and checked again. Yes, they'd been thorough, taking every last dime. They took my wallet, too, but true to my word, there were no credit cards in there—I've never had a credit card. I have no credit history.

And my phone. They took my phone.

I did another few minutes of unrestrained breathing. It felt pretty good.

I didn't remember doing it, but before hell broke out, I must have stuck the key in the ignition. I turned it. There was a half-second of hesitation, then the car came to life. I drove. So I had a car and a set of keys, and that was about all. The muggers had taken my own keys so I couldn't even easily get back into my apartment. The building manager would let me in, but I'd have to pay to get a new lock put in, and lose my deposit—honestly right then I didn't recall how that worked. The crooks had taken the other wallet—the one from the dead man in the men's room—which wrecked the idea of going to his place and taking what was there of value—I didn't have an address.

"Hold on there, buddy," I told myself in a delightful western twang I'd been working up. At the next red light I reached over and popped open the glove box. There was a registration slip inside and an insurance card, both with the men's room druggy's name and address. I was only about ten blocks away, in the East Hollywood, Silverlake, Echo Park direction. If I was lucky this guy lived in Los Feliz and was loaded, or if not, he'd have more of his drugs stashed there.

It turned out to be an adobe building, a tenement, ten to twenty units housing a few hundred recent arrivals from various Latin American shitholes crammed into small spaces along with a hefty minority of near-homeless gringos, many young, many addicted, if I can be allowed that observation. I drove the car past, took a look, and parked a block away, in case my men's room friend had any other friends among the *campesinos* hanging out on the front stoop.

They gave me some looks, but nobody said anything as I entered and climbed the stairs, up to 3B, the room on the car registration. I started to use the key when I heard noise from inside—shouting and a TV. Another couple was in there; that hadn't even occurred to me.

I could come back, I supposed, when they weren't there—

Curious residents stuck their necks out of half the apartments on the floor, utilizing some kind of innate "stranger on the floor" radar poor people seem to always possess. It's the same in my building, the Arbuckle, I have to admit.

I could knock, ask if "Hamilton" was there—that was the name from the glove compartment, but then maybe they'd known him as "Ham" or "Skip" or would suspect me of being a narc—by the sound of their voices, these were rough, angry people.

"I don't have to put up with this," I stated firmly to myself, pivoting to the stairs. "I do not have to stoop this low. I do not have to descend to breaking and entering and common thievery."

I marched out of the place with my head held high, and strolled down the block to dead Ham's Nissan, which started right up again—"don't call *this* a piece of shit"—and started driving west back to Hollywood. I checked the gas, which I hadn't done before. Nearly a full tank.

"Things are looking up, Jackie-boy," I drawled.

I refused to feel sorry for myself. I was a victim, for sure. A victim of our horrible educational system where ignorant, unread hoodlums roam the streets, breaking into apartments, where if you have $35,000 in cash you don't dare leave it at home when you go out, and what about our banking system? Where you can't just go in and deposit that kind of cash money without filling out all sorts of forms and attracting attention from government regulators. And forget about opening a bank account anyway without six forms of ID and a permanent address and a credit card—

Don't get me started.

I was enjoying the scenery—that was enough for the moment. I didn't get this far east on Sunset that often.

I went to see Rayna.

Izzy heard me pull up. He answered the door himself. It had one of those iron-bar things outside the wood door, very decorative, hand-welded no doubt but still in the style of the house. I could see it was locked tight and there was no way I'd get inside uninvited, but there were big spaces between the bars if somebody wanted to shoot Izzy or throw a knife and get him that way. I made a note to myself to learn to do that—

"How'd you get in here?" Izzy demanded to know.

"The gate was open."

That was true, and I could see it bothered Izzy greatly that he'd forgotten something and wasn't all perfect.

"What do you want?" he asked gruffly.

"I want to speak to Rayna," I told him.

"She's not here," he replied.

"She's right there," I pointed out, as she appeared a dozen yards down the hall, staying in the shadows.

"She doesn't want to talk to you," Izzy told me.

"Why don't we ask her?" I suggested.

I could see that made Izzy angry. I could also see there was nothing I could do about it right then, not until I'd taken my knife-throwing lessons, and there'd probably be a lot of practice involved, I was pretty sure. I wondered who gave that kind of instruction. You can find an instructor for anything in Hollywood—riding, roping, guitar, piano, voice, dialects, guns, knives, swords and spears, you name it. I could also see that if Izzy was angry he'd take it out on Rayna, and that was something I didn't want.

"Okay, I'll leave you two love-birds alone," I grinned, holding up my hands. "I just wanted to wish you all the best. No harm, no foul, right? Sorry to disturb."

I got back into that piece of shit car and wished I'd stolen something better for this occasion. I'd faked an apology, but that didn't mean I didn't have some pride. Of course that bastard Izzy had a narrow Beverly Hills driveway and I hadn't really planned it right and instead of backing all the way out past the gates to the street, I thought I could do a three-point turn and head out straight, but of course I got stuck that way between low stone walls on each side, just high enough that you couldn't quite see them over the hood in front and trunk in back, and I only had a few inches leeway, inching back and forth over and over, turning the squeaky wheel back and forth till my arms ached—no power steering, of course—with the stinking car not running that well now and Izzy laughing at the door, and Rayna, too, probably.

By the time I got out of there, I was ready to murder somebody.

I picked Jaime.

CHAPTER 18

Larry Gregg had to admit the place gave him the creeps. It wasn't just the time difference, or the people's indifference, or the lack of...Gregg couldn't put his finger on it. "Moral compass" is what the politicians would call it. To Gregg it was more like "meaning" or "purpose."

Gregg himself hadn't led a perfect life, that was certain. But he'd studied as hard as he could in school, competed in every sporting event to the best of his ability, "protected and served" on the police force, tried to uphold the law and maybe stem the tide of violence and degradation anybody with eyes could see. Here, in Hollywood, he wasn't so sure what was important, not even to him. He tried to sleep on it, as tired as he was, but his mind in a half-dream always came back to the lobby of the Arbuckle Apartments. It had unnerved him, like a rat trapped in a maze observed from a high angle with a wide, fish-eye lens, both dark and over-lit, bright bulbs flaring into the camera like an episode of *The Twilight Zone* (1959-1964).

You're creeping yourself out, Gregg told himself. *It's all in your head.*

"There are eight million stories in the naked city," Gregg muttered, "and this is one of them."

That was it—*Naked City* (1948)—Gregg had loved that film. He'd seen it as a kid late at night on TV. Black and white, gritty streets, tough talk. Maybe it was why Gregg had become a detective, along with other films like it. Gregg looked it up and wrote it down: "*Naked City* (1948)." Later, he'd check if it was on Netflix or Amazon or Hulu or something.

Life is so much easier now, isn't it? he mused.

Gregg wouldn't look up the film right then; he knew that would be a mistake. It would be readily available as an illegal stream on YouTube and he'd no doubt watch the whole thing and not get any sleep. He noticed they'd made a TV series of it, too, on for four years, back when a season was thirty-five episodes, not just thirteen.

You might not sleep for a month.

Gregg felt guilty for watching things for free. He knew there were living, breathing people who made their living in the film industry. He'd seen them walking around Hollywood. He marveled at the effort. Los Angeles, he had realized in just a few days, wasn't just rich people, fancy cars, sunshine, beaches and stars. It was a real working town where people did their best to get up in the morning and go to their jobs and put food on the table for their families. That part was familiar, like Minnesota or Wisconsin or Kansas, which wasn't surprising—that's where most of those same people came from originally.

But now you didn't have to go to the movies to see one; you could rent one off the internet or see a million at no charge on the internet if you knew how to look, or on your phone, or computer, or on your watch. It cheapened the whole thing in Detective Gregg's mind.

What did Norma Desmond say in Sunset Boulevard (1950)?

"I *am* big! It's the pictures that got small!"

She had no idea...

Gregg wondered how those massive studios he'd seen around town would ever survive—Warners, Disney, Paramount, Sony. Would they go under and crumble, blown into thin air like MySpace and AOL? Or would they live on like the pyramids of Egypt, a testament to human ego and greed?

The Ten Commandments (1956). Cecil B. Demille...

"The stuff that dreams are made of," according to Sam Spade in *The Maltese Falcon* (1941).

Gregg fell soundly asleep.

———•—•———

The next day, Larry Gregg caught Lowanna Xanderson's young receptionist coming out of the building. He trailed her down the street to a small cafe at the end of the block. Gregg reminded himself that he had never been much good at a tail—

Sure enough, the receptionist turned suddenly and caught Larry Gregg following.

"Should I call the cops?" she wanted to know.

"Please don't. I just want to talk to you."

"I'm on lunch-break."

"I'll buy," Gregg offered.

"Deal," the receptionist told him.

They sat and looked at a menu and ordered.

"I'm Larry Gregg," the detective offered, handing her his hand.

"I know—you gave me your card before," the receptionist said.

Again, Gregg's breath was taken away by how devastatingly cute she was. Not beautiful exactly, but cute—

Like a puppy...

"And you are...?" Gregg tried.

"No names," the woman answered. "I won't give you my name. I could get in all sorts of trouble. I could lose my job. It's a crappy job but that's better than no job. You know what it's like not to have a job in this town? No money, no credibility, nobody to help you. People *shun* you—that's what they do. It's like the fucking Scarlet Letter—that's what it's like. You ever read that book?"

"No."

"Pretty nasty stuff, trust me. They made into a movie like ten times, none of them any good, except I like the Meg Foster version a lot. She's got those weird blue eyes you just want to stare at all day. I'm thinking about getting contacts. Or something. Eyes are the thing. Like Karen Black. Cross-eyed her whole career. Didn't hurt her a bit. You a big movie fan, Mr. Detective from the badlands?"

"I am, actually," Larry Gregg replied.

"Good. You gotta be in this town. Everybody here is movie crazy. And sex. So where you're from, it's just like *Fargo* (1996), isn't it?"

"They pretty much nailed it," Gregg affirmed.

"I thought so," the woman replied.

"Did you show her the pictures?" Gregg asked.

"What pictures?" the girl complained, sounding much younger, annoyed, a tantrum.

"The pictures of Julie Baker, aka Rayna Rourke."

"Yeah, I showed her," the receptionist spat out. "I could lose my job. I could be homeless by the end of the month. She doesn't even want me talking to you. 'You see this man again, you don't talk to him, understand?' That's what Low said to me."

"Low?"

"Lowanna Xanderson, the agent—that's who we're talking about here, isn't it? Are you even paying attention here?"

"I'm sorry—"

"I have half a mind to take you over my knee, buster," the young receptionist spat out, "and spank your bare bottom red and raw—you'd like that wouldn't you, Mr. 'I'm just all Cookies and Milk and a Farm boy from the Sticks'—wouldn't you?"

Larry Gregg couldn't help it. His face turned beet-red.

The girl laughed.

The food came. She dug in eagerly. Gregg played with his omelet.

"Call me Wanda," she said, mouth full, still finding Gregg's chagrin amusing.

"So Lowanna seemed to know Julie Baker?" Gregg tried.

"Sure did."

"And so did you," Gregg guessed.

"Bingo," Wanda answered.

"You were upset at the photos," Gregg observed, "when I showed them to you the first time."

"Yeah, I was upset. I had Rayna in the files and I gave your friend her information. I shouldn't have but he seemed nice enough and he caught me at a vulnerable moment but let's not go into that right now."

Larry Gregg wanted desperately to know what that meant, what that "vulnerable moment" was—would his friend, George Landon, happily married, four decades older, have succumbed to the charms of this young siren?

Vixen, tramp, tease, kinky dinky—funny words danced in his head. But he let her speak:

"I was pretty sure your detective buddy raped and killed Rayna and it was my fault."

Gregg put down his fork with a clang and leaned back in his chair, stunned by the statement, like an uppercut to the chin. The bellyache would come later.

"What...what makes you say that...?" he asked.

"Just a feeling I had, that's all, when you asked me. It went away quickly enough, believe me. It was stupid. Your friend was a nice guy—he wouldn't do that. Though it takes all kinds, doesn't it? Y-N-K, that's my motto."

"Y-N-K?"

"You never know."

"Oh."

"Your friend doesn't go around killing people, right?" Wanda asked.

"No, I assure you, no."

"Glad to hear it," Wanda replied. "Listen, I don't usually order dessert..."

"Please, go ahead," Gregg told her. "On me. Anything you want."

The detective watched Wanda eat overpriced cheesecake while he quizzed her about her interaction with George Landon. He established that she only saw him one time, at the agency, and she'd given him the phone number and address of "Rayna Rourke" because he'd convinced her she was missing and her parents were worried about her. That was the only time Wanda had spoken to Landon, she claimed—

"I didn't shack up with the guy or meet him for drinks or anything like that," Wanda assured Greg, "but you're right, I *am* that kind of girl."

The redness came back into Gregg's face. He liked Wanda. He was horribly attracted to her, even if her favorite thing to do was shock him and make him squirm like he was some rube from the sticks, which he realized he *was* based on exactly how he was acting.

"Just...just how kinky are you?" Larry Gregg asked as he walked her back to her place of employment. If she'd been involved with Rayna and there'd been some kind of rough sex—

"Relax, cowboy," Wanda answered. "Nothing you can't handle—"

"That's not why I asked—"

"And I don't know anything about Rayna and although I'm pretty sure she's dead, I don't know anything about it. We didn't team up for threesome orgies at stars' pool parties or anything like that, if that's what your dirty little mind is thinking."

"I wasn't thinking that," Gregg lied.

Wanda laughed.

"Now you stay right here," she said, "while I go the other way, okay? I can't be seen with you." She lowered her voice. "But if you want to call... we can go line-dancing or hay-riding or horseshoes or whatever the fuck you guys do, okay?"

Wanda marched off.

Larry Gregg watched her go, halfway in love.

"It's Hollywood Boulevard, Jake..."

He looked down. Carole Lombard. Out of respect, he stepped off her star.

CHAPTER 19

I'm not a genius, nor am I a criminal mastermind. I'm just a guy who figured out that if Jaime Rojo de Luna had thirty-five thousand dollars in cash in his little cubby-hole office to pay for a Ferrari, he might have more there and I could take it and wouldn't need to steal another car to get it. The fact I'd have to kill Jaime just made it all the more delightful. The guy had dissed me too many times, I figured, and deserved it.

I parked down the street and walked up. Jaime's place was pretty quiet. The gates were closed, with a big padlock. Fortunately for me there were no dogs. I could climb the fence, no problem, but it might make a racket and wake Jaime up—

I looked at my watch: 3 am. He just might be so asleep not to notice.

Then there was the razor wire—

I got back into the Nissan and drove around a little, to a residential area, and found just what I was looking for, a hill of discarded carpeting put out at the curb. It was nasty stuff, and I hated to even touch it, but my disgust at the carpeting paled in comparison to my disgust at my circumstances, and I intended to do something about that.

I loaded as much of the ripped-out carpeting as would fit into the back seat and trunk of the Nissan and drove back to Jaime's little compound. This time I threw the car into neutral and cut the engine halfway down the block and coasted up to the "auto-repair" shop. No way was I going to drag all that rancid carpeting down the sidewalk.

I'm not a body-builder but I'm young and strong—I insist on it, and it wasn't much of a problem to climb up the chain-link fence and toss the carpet remnants over the razor-wire on top. After a half-dozen trips, slowly, careful not to make any noise, I had erected a very nice six-foot long bed over the top. I spent no time congratulating myself, but tested the contraption right away, crawling over the carpet and into the compound. Ostensibly an auto repair facility, there were car-parts strewn around, and a couple of obviously disabled vehicles with layers of San Fernando dust stuck to them. The real treasures would be inside the two locked garages—the Ferrari might even still be in one of them. I would check that. After...

The door to Jaime's little office/living quarters was locked, but only the knob, and there was a wide divot where someone had chipped away the wood to break in previously, possibly Jaime himself if he'd lost the key. I had my knife out already, of course, and it made quick work of the obstacle.

Darkness was my main enemy then, and I was essentially blind, like that scene in *Wait Until Dark* (1967), Audrey Hepburn's best picture, I think. I'm not a big Hepburn fan. Most men aren't. Women love her. Men prefer something meatier, like Ingrid Bergman. Bergman would have been good in that movie, too, but she might also have beat the crap out of Alan Arkin and Richard Crenna at her very first suspicion, which would have been a different movie, I suppose. Vulnerable, my ass.

Anyway, it was pitch-black, as they say.

I didn't kill Jaime Rojo de Luna, his sleep apnea did. They say it's a deadly affliction. The snoring told me right where he was, on a little cot in the next room, with a desk, a computer, a hotplate and a printer, and that was about all. I'd have to figure out where the money was afterwards. There was no safe.

I stabbed him first, right in the chest, which woke him up so he could scream and be appropriately shocked at who was killing him. The blood sprayed everywhere, like a fountain, so I had to slit his throat quickly, from ear to ear, and then he hardly made a sound, just some gurgling and his legs kicked and his arms flew out, which I found startling and disturbing, but you learn to be surprised when doing this sort of thing, without letting it affect your work.

I turned on the lights, put on latex gloves, and searched the room. As I figured, he kept a pistol under his pillow, and some other weapons around the room. I'm glad I hadn't awakened him; it would have been bad news for me. The money, about $50,000, was right on his desk. There was no attempt to hide it. If he had more money hidden somewhere on the premises, I didn't find it in the time allotted—I allowed myself just one hour to search. I was tired, I have to admit, after all the adventures of the evening, and despite the thrill of the kill, I could drop off to sleep at any moment.

I checked the garages. Unfortunately, they were empty. No exotic cars, nothing to steal. Maybe for the best; Jaime was the only hot-car customer I knew anyway, and I had decided I'd get out of that business. Too tired to climb back over the fence, which is probably what I should have done, I went back into the office and found a ring of keys, one of which fit the enormous padlock on the front gate. I locked the lock again on my way out and took the keys with me. At the least, it might delay the finding of the body, and at best, it would really cheese off the cops, not being able to get into anything easily on the premises.

I really wanted to take Jaime with me, strip him down to the bones and eat his meaty flesh for the next month or so—I was getting a little tired of Helen Majors, I have to admit. She was tasty but I was ready for a change.

The guy just weighed too much. The cocaine from the bathroom had worn off and as I say, I was frankly exhausted by the driving around and the stabbing and all of it. It's not easy doing what I do.

So I just took his arm. Cut it off from the shoulder and wrapped it up in some clear plastic and heaved it over the fence before escaping myself. Crazy, impulsive—what can I say? That's how I am.

Dawn was just breaking as I neared the Arbuckle Apartments. I found a place to park a quarter mile away and said farewell to the Nissan, leaving it open and the keys in the ignition. If somebody stole it and drove it around for a year or two, that would be just fine with me.

I slung Jaime's arm over my shoulder and walked toward the sun and marveled at how clean and fresh the city could look in the morning. Later, it would be hot, and windy, and the smells would rise up from the pavement, and the air would fill with whatever pollutant ruled that day, but right then, life was perfect. Because of the clear plastic, it was obvious I was strolling down the street with a human arm over my shoulder and flopping down my back, blood dripping on the stars on Hollywood Boulevard, but the few pedestrians I passed and nobody in their cars mentioned it, or seemed to care. That's life in the big city, nonchalant, jaded, "can't faze me." Wonderful, isn't it? I think so.

I laughed, thinking back to a book I once read, *Day of the Locust* by Nathanael West. There's a guy in there who comes to Hollywood to make it big but instead keeps losing his limbs—arms, legs, one by one. Me? I'm *gaining* body parts! Ha!

Perhaps it was the exhaustion, a "runner's high" that made me feel that way, but when my giddy, giggly head hit the pillow, I was instantly asleep, the joy of living on this great Earth, this wonderful country, this fabulous city, flooding over me like a warm Malibu wave.

CHAPTER 20

Hack Jamison was a detective but just barely, and he knew it. Considered a hothead and a ticking time-bomb ready to go off at any moment, on suspension three times in the last year, he was no doubt destined for early retirement at the age of thirty if the brass had anything to say about it.

The first thing they'd done was to strip him of his body-cam at the advice of the LAPD lawyers. A straight-out firing wasn't an option (yet)—the cops' union was closely monitoring the case and threatened legal action.

But what Jamison's supervisors *could* do is what they did: assign him to the Stolen Vehicle Task Force, a dead-end down a cul-de-sac down a rabbit-hole career track.

This morning, Jamison was driving an unmarked Ford-something— "whatever's left on the lot the other detectives don't want"—to an impound lot in Venice, a mile from the beach.

"At least it'll be cool down there," Jamison told himself. This morning's task was to take a look at a silver-gray-beige, seven-year-old Chrysler 300 with no plates left abandoned on Sawtelle and Charnock, under the 405 freeway, towed after an initial ticketing and then the 72-hour limit. Jamison's job was to inspect the vehicle, write down the VIN number, check the trunk, etc., for dead bodies, contraband, weapons, etc., then file the paperwork. Other detectives—"the real ones"—would take it from there, tracking down the owner, checking it against the stolen-car registry nationwide, finger-printing it if necessary. Nine times out of ten an abandoned vehicle—even one this new—was just that, abandoned, after it broke down, its owner too lazy, too stupid, or just too slow about doing something about it. Even in LA (maybe *especially* in LA) some people put their cars in the same category as the couches, shopping carts, and big-screen TVs left on the curb for weeks on end.

Jamison parked in the yellow zone outside the impound lot. Once a scary alley in an industrial part of Venice just east of Lincoln, the lot itself was now easily valued at three million, recently surrounded by trendy condos and overbuilt mid-century modern mansions. Marina Del Rey sat just a block to the south. Still, the auto impound lot stayed put—"Auction Every Thursday—Cash Only"—populated by a mix of vehicles towed from all over the west side.

"Hey, Ralph," Jamison checked in at the bullet-proof window.

"Hey, boss," Ralph answered. He called everyone "boss." Jamison suspected it was because he couldn't remember anyone's name. "You here about the Chrysler?"

"You got it," Jamison answered.

Ralph buzzed Jamison in past the chain-link and barbed wire.

"Straight back," Ralph advised.

"Thanks," the detective answered, and surfed through the various vehicles to his target.

The thing had been there a week, according to records, and was covered in dust—the drought continued. Jamison put on gloves and checked the doors—all locked. He popped the driver's side with a Slim Jim, then opened the trunk with the lever inside.

Better to get it over with, Jamison decided with a mix of excitement and revulsion. There was always the chance of a dead body or bodies in the trunk. If that was the case, it would put Jamison right smack in the middle of a homicide case, perhaps resurrecting his failing career, even if he *was* under strict and explicit orders not to touch anything if it might involve a serious crime. They'd want homicide in there—"not your sorry ass, Jamison."

There was nothing in the trunk, absolutely nothing, which meant it had been picked clean, no doubt, while sitting on the street. The fact the car still had its wheels was a lucky break, but also a testament to the glut of automotive merchandise on the market.

"People like the custom rims these days," was the general feeling in law enforcement, a trend which had decidedly reduced the detectives' work-load.

Inside the car was the same story—someone had removed everything, quickly, loaded it into a bag, no doubt, in the dark of night to sift through later.

Jamison got down on his knees and felt under the passenger's seat, coming up with a forgotten registration, three years old, from this same car—he checked the VIN number against the one on the dash—registered in Minnesota to a certain George Landon with an address in Minneapolis.

"Bingo," Jamison couldn't help announcing.

Suddenly, his Motorola squawked on his shoulder—a rare, almost unheard-of occurrence since being assigned to Stolen Vehicle.

"You there, Jamison?" the dispatcher demanded.

"I'm here," Jamison answered.

"You've been reassigned."

Jamison swallowed hard. *What could be worse? The jail? Foot patrol on Skid Row?*

"Okay..." Jamison answered. If he quit, he wasn't sure what he'd do. *Security guard?*

"It's all hands on deck in the stolen car arena, apparently," the dispatcher stated. "Jaime Rojo de Luna's been gunned down at his place in the valley."

"Jaime Rojo de Luna?" Jamison repeated.

The man was famous, a legend in the stolen vehicle arena—

"That's what I said, isn't it?" the dispatcher came back. "You're to report immediately. I'm texting the address to your vehicle."

Jamison's heart rose in his chest and a grin ached on his face. He pocketed the registration slip on the Chrysler, shut the doors but did not lock them, and headed straight for the exit to the impound lot.

"One other thing," the dispatcher added, chuckling.

"What's that?"

"You still got your service revolver, right?"

"Yes," Jamison replied, checking his hip to be sure.

"They told me to be sure to tell you to put that in the glove compartment of your vehicle and lock it there."

"Ha ha," Jamison replied.

"They weren't actually kidding about that, bro," the dispatcher noted. "You're going to be tagging stolen vehicles, checking VINs, that's it. Got it?"

Jamison didn't answer.

"Over and out," the dispatcher concluded, hanging up.

Fuming, Jamison hurried to his car.

CHAPTER 21

The way Izzy Clurman was playing the part of the asshole movie producer in *The Canyons* (2013) was starting to bug me.

Every night I'd go spy on him as he arranged more threesomes with Rayna plus one more random guy off the streets. How he found so many good-looking actors who were *straight* is beyond me, ha ha. It was only a matter of time before other women would show up, too, I figured, or toys, equipment—people want new things night after night. They get bored. But not me. I watched from the side of the hill or up a tree. Meanwhile he cheated on her like crazy, I noticed, sneaking women into the house behind her back when she was asleep. It was kind of breathtaking.

Even more disturbing was the fact Izzy didn't let Rayna leave the house. Her car wasn't even there and he never let her drive one of his.

I watched it night after night. I let it go on and didn't interfere. I wasn't going to get in touch with her. I wasn't going to play the part of the old scraggly broke-ass actor boyfriend like in the *Canyons* movie, which BTW is Paul Schrader's worst film. Probably *anybody's* worst film, but then again, I *like* pictures about womanizing creeps, even though I don't really consider them creeps, just men—like me—who know what they want. What's unrealistic is the guy always gets his come-uppance in the movies, and is horribly hurt one way or another at the end, if not dead. In my experience, that doesn't need to happen, not if a guy follows the tenets of my program. It's like root-canal for the soul—you drill deep and grind out all the pain and emotion, fears and desires. After that you bite down on life and chew it up and suck out all its juices and it doesn't hurt a bit. We're infected with "feelings"—which, let's face it, are nothing but torture and agony.

The Zens know this. They get there with the praying and the meditation and the yoga and shit, if they get to it at all.

My way's quicker. The Skullys taught me. Erase your conscience. Thoroughly. Completely. Soldiers do this. Executioners do this. Statesmen do this.

So that's my take on *The Canyons* (2013), not recommended. The main character is named Christian. You ever notice that? If a guy's a real creep in a movie, his name is Christian. Somebody should look into that—part of the War on Christmas, no doubt. Like a big fat guy is always called "Tiny" for some reason. Misplaced irony, that's what it is. Save your irony for when you really need it, I say.

So Izzy and his hired hands did it up proud to Rayna every night and they generally left her bruised and battered, but that's show business, right?

I told myself, "This is the good part, really. I can watch, I can get off, I don't have to do anything or spend any money or get caught in all that 'relationship' crap. Izzy and Rayna do it for me. Then I go home and fill my guts eating the power of my victims and they make me strong."

I wasn't jealous of Izzy, or of his male friends. It wasn't in me.

Freddy Weaver was another story. The picture of that wrinkled old fucker plowing my Rayna stuck in my head. When Freddy told that cop that he'd done that, it was all I could do to keep from killing him on the spot. Fortunately my P-E-A-C-E training kicked in along with I-P-T-B-C. I paused, stayed cautious, and lived to fight another day. Maybe this was the day—

"I'm sorry," Freddy Weaver told me when I showed up for class, making no attempt to take me aside and speak to me privately, "you haven't paid your fees for this month. I'm going to have to ask you to leave."

The other actors scattered after hearing this. It was obvious Freddy was making an example of me, warning the others through me. That's what made me the angriest. *They* at least understood I was dangerous.

"I'll pay you," I mumbled.

"Now? Are you prepared to pay now?" he asked.

I pulled out my wallet, thick with Jaime's bills, some still sticky from his blood. Not the way I like to do things, but stuff happens, you know? I counted out three hundreds and shoved them into Freddy's chest.

"Here's your goddamn money," I hissed at him.

I could see he was scared. I liked that. I would have killed him right then and there except the money was in my right hand and my knife was in the right pocket—

Freddy fixed that himself by prying the bills from my fingers.

"I will need next month as well," he said, "in advance."

I glared. I considered.

"You know," I told the weasel, "I'm not sure I'm getting that much out of this class."

"If you're not, it's because you're not listening, or working on your scenes, or putting in the time—"

"Maybe it's because you're a piece-of-shit teacher," I replied.

He laughed. A big mistake. You don't laugh at an angry person, the same way you don't tell them to "calm down."

I *had* put in the time, especially on my own self-awareness, self-empowering program, The J-C-C Method, and without that I would have killed the guy on the spot, no doubt.

So I went and got drunk. I'm not a good drunk. I have to admit that. I get angry. I need to work on that—anger is a luxury for losers.

CHAPTER 22

They had it all wrong, Detective Jamison noted when he arrived at the scene of Jaime Rojo's murder. The man hadn't been "gunned down;" he'd been killed with a knife, throat slit, nearly decapitated.

"Typical," Jamison muttered to himself, standing outside the yellow crime tape *like a goddamn civilian.*

Also, Jaime's arm was missing.

In addition, to everyone's surprise, there were no cars there, stolen or otherwise, and there was nothing much for Detective Jamison to do. Finally, after an hour of waiting while the homicide squad and the coroner's men and the computer forensics guys (like everybody, Jaime had a computer) went through the office and the empty garages, the lead detective came out with a piece of paper and called Jamison over.

"I need you to go out and check out these addresses," the detective told Jamison. "Our dead man owned these properties, it looks like. See what's there. Break a lock if you have to, but that's it, okay? Don't touch anything, just give me the preliminary. We'll have the team out there eventually; we just need to know the score."

Jamison took the piece of paper. It had a half-dozen addresses on it, all in the Santa Clarita area, up the Newhall Pass and over the mountains. At the bottom:

"That's my personal number," the lead detective told Jamison. "Call when you're done, or call if you find something important before you're done, understand?"

Jamison nodded. They were treating him like an idiot. That was okay, he decided. He'd show them.

"Boutros Boutros Golly!" Jamison declared when he opened the first warehouse door, invoking both the name of the sixth Secretary-General of the United Nations and a twenty-five-year-old episode of *Seinfeld* (1989-1998).

There were Jaguars inside, Bugattis, Mercedes, Corvettes, Mustangs, MGs, muscle-cars and race cars, Alfas and hot-rods—

This is like Jay fucking Leno's garage...

In the next split second, an impure thought entered Detective Jamison's mind. There were twenty-five cars here, at least, each worth a hundred grand minimum.

"*You* do the math," Jamison whispered. All he had to do was call it in: "Sorry, boss, no cars here," and it would probably be a week, if ever, before they sent somebody else to verify. By then Jamison could drive every one to a new location. He was in the business of stolen cars, after all—admittedly on the law enforcement side—but he had a good idea of the process to get the merchandise sold and out of the country and placed overseas, and he knew the players—minus Jaime Rojo now—and he knew everybody in stolen cars on the force, undercover or not—

CHAPTER 23

You're probably wondering why I left Jaime's guns with his dead body:

My rules: no guns. Too easy, impersonal, no fun. You gotta deal with a bunch of losers anyway—short guys with tiny dicks who run the gun-shops, the sporting-goods departments, the shooting ranges—same guys who used to sell auto parts, or plumbing supplies—they're the worst: "I'm a licensed plumber and you're not and you don't have a fucking idea what you're doing, do you?"

Who needs 'em. Fuck 'em, I say. A knife is more fun every time and it doesn't make much noise, not if you use it right.

Second rule: a reason. No random killings. That guy who killed 90 in the news—he got away with it because there was no reason whatsoever. He got off on it, that's all. Strictly sex, nothing more. Okay, I got that prob-lem, too, but I have other motives, more important motives. Science, for one. Anatomy, chemistry, forensics—I'm learning all that shit. Jaime's guns could have been connected to who-knows-what crimes in the past. I could get picked up and charged with things so far from my experience it'd be a huge joke, but which the criminal justice system might take very seriously.

Strangers on a Train (1951). Still valid. If you want to get away with killing people for no reason whatsoever. Not me. I need a reason.

The day after Jaime's untimely demise, an envelope arrived from Oregon. It looked official enough and I recognized the address. My hands shook as I opened it and took out the document. It was my birth certifi-cate—it said so right up at the top. I looked to the date—the same one I'd

117

been celebrating every year since I could remember. It's amazing how good seeing your birthday written down makes you feel. It's like hearing your own name spoken.

And there it was, my name: "Porter Monroe Skully," right there. Under "Mother," it said "Mary Rosalie Skully," and under "Father" was written "Michael James Skully." I jumped up and paced the room, pumping my fist in celebration. This was documentary proof of my name, which the other actor had stolen from me, which he paid dearly for, with his life, and which now I would reclaim—

I paused. Something wasn't right. I looked at the sheet of paper again, trying to justify my doubt, reconcile my apprehension—

The State of Oregon was saying that my natural parents were Mack and Rose Skully!

A lie! A damned lie!

I was an orphan, I was certain. No way those two yokels could have born me. Not a chance I had a single strand of DNA in me of any relation to those two!

I kept circling the room, trying to make sense of what I had known all my life. It could not have been a mistake. This was intentional. The fix was in. My original birth had been erased, replaced with this sham—

The vastness of the conspiracy overwhelmed me. I sat down hard. I knew then I was part of some diabolical experiment like *Re-Animator* (1985), *Boys from Brazil* (1978), *Eternal Sunshine* (2004), *Truman Show* (1998), (how come Jim Carrey's in *both* of those?)—

I had to laugh. It explained it all. I was not responsible for my own actions. I no longer possessed Free Will. I was being manipulated by others for their own purposes. Of course I wasn't Mack and Rose's kid; I was the product of a laboratory, a test to see what I would do...

I didn't intend to disappoint them.

The birth certificate did put a new spin on my quest for my heritage. I now knew the journey would be long and arduous, with formidable obstacles placed in my way, powerful forces aligned against me. The conspiracy no doubt reached into the highest echelons of world government, to the seats of power, like every 80s thriller made.

It wouldn't be easy—nothing worthwhile is—but I was up for it. In fact, I was just the man to do it.

CHAPTER 24

Larry Gregg's hands shook holding the phone. He couldn't remember being this nervous. He'd even written down all his lines and rehearsed them over and over, affecting a southern accent to disguise his voice. He'd also wrapped the cell-phone in a handkerchief to further change things around, just in case. Still, Gregg suffered from stage fright. Here he was in the center of Hollywood, surrounded by the greatest actors in the world, yet he couldn't—

The idea wrote itself, Larry Gregg realized. He hopped out of his car and walked the block down to Hollywood Boulevard.

Throw a rock and you're bound to hit a dozen actors, he figured. It wasn't *quite* that easy. He needed young and male for the role. Two screenwriters and a wannabe rock star later, he found his actor, and agreed on a $20 fee for five minutes work.

"Just read this," Gregg directed when they'd found a quiet residential street well off the boulevard.

"Hello," the actor read into the phone, "I'm Ms. Xanderson's driver tonight for the premiere and I'm afraid I've misplaced the vital information. Would you please...?"

The receptionist replied sharply—it was Wanda; Gregg recognized the voice as he leaned his ear in close. She proceeded to ream out Gregg, vowing to get him fired.

"Please," the actor ad-libbed, "I really need this job and I think I remember but I want to confirm—"

Wanda again read him the riot act, but in the end she told Gregg and his talented young actor what Gregg wanted to know: where and when to pick her up for the screening that night.

Detective Gregg rented a black Lincoln Town Car and a black suit too—it turned out you could rent almost anything in Hollywood, from a grip truck to a palm tree to a fully accurate 747 interior.

Gregg arrived at the office early and called up from the street.

"Miss Xanderson's ride is here," Gregg said simply, hoping Wanda the receptionist wouldn't remember the actor's voice from earlier in the day or Gregg's own voice from the previous day.

Gregg got out of the car and opened the door for Ms. Xanderson as he waited for her to arrive. He tried to affect the same mix of arrogance, elegance, subservience and "fuck you" he'd seen on other servants of the super-rich, from *Upstairs, Downstairs* (1971-1975) and *Downton Abbey* (2010-2015) mostly.

Lowanna Xanderson wasn't quite what Gregg had expected. She was shorter for one thing, and humbler, saying "thank you so much" as Gregg helped her into the car.

"Busy" seemed to fit her as she compulsively worked her phone—texting, then calling—"This is Lowanna. Got your message. The answer is 'let me think about it.'"

Gregg drove, hoping for an opening. The premiere was in Westwood, right next to UCLA, starring a young client of the agent's—Kenny Jarman—an up-and-comer, "star of tomorrow"—there was "Oscar buzz."

"Miss Xanderson?" Gregg tried when Ms. Xanderson looked up from her phone for a second, catching Gregg's eyes in the rear-view mirror.

Gregg had taken Wilshire, a rookie mistake no real chauffeur would have made—a parking lot this time of the evening on a week-day.

"Yes?" Ms. Xanderson replied.

"There's something you should know about me."

"Is that right?" she said, that sympathetic demeanor Gregg first noticed suddenly *Gone with the Wind* (1939). She'd been here before; she knew the drill. Later, she'd call the company and get the chauffeur fired for being way out of line.

"I'm not really a chauffeur," Larry Gregg told the agent.

"Is that right?" she answered.

Gregg glanced in the rear-view mirror, failing to catch her rolling eyes, but he could tell by the sound of her voice—

"Let me guess," Lowanna Xanderson declared, "you're really an actor."

"No, I'm not an actor," Gregg chuckled.

Lowanna was clearly skeptical.

"I'm a detective," he said.

"Okay, that's it. Let me out. I'll get a ride somehow. Where are we?"

"I'll take you to your premiere—I really will. I just want some information on a Julie Baker, who you know as Rayna Rourke," Gregg spoke quickly, forcefully.

In the back seat, Lowanna sunk into her seat.

"Why?" she asked.

"Her parents are worried about her," Gregg answered.

"Is that who you work for, her parents?" Lowanna asked.

"Exactly."

"Where? Where are her parents?"

"Wisconsin."

Lowanna exhaled again. Gregg reached into his jacket and pulled out his detective's card and the letter signed by the Baker parents authorizing him to look for their child.

Ms. Xanderson studied the documents carefully. She was convinced, but still not happy.

"Is this what you do—sneak around lying to people, pretending to be something you're not?" Lowanna challenged, clearly upset.

"You wouldn't talk to me—"

"I'm a busy person—"

"We have time now!" Gregg bellowed. He was getting impatient. His friend George Landon would have knocked her block off already.

"She's fine. Rayna is absolutely fine. She's very safe—I'm making sure of that," Lowanna told the detective.

"Well that's nice," Gregg answered sarcastically. "I'm sure her parents will be fucking thrilled to hear you say that."

"Listen, mister—"

"No, you listen!" Gregg shouted, hitting the brakes, jerking the car to the curb, turning to read her the riot act—

Lowanna jumped out of the car, not interested—

Horns blared. Gregg rushed out of the Lincoln in bumper-to-bumper traffic, Wilshire Boulevard and Beverly Glen. Already a Sigalert was in the works and the traffic helicopters headed that way. WAZE directed traffic north up the narrow side-streets east of the UCLA campus. Gregg would have followed Ms. Xanderson in the car, but she backtracked and headed north on Le Conte on foot and there was no way Gregg could turn around and get to her. He was lucky no one ran him over.

"That's okay," the detective muttered to himself, "I know where she's going."

Gregg pulled up in front of the theatre in a "no parking" zone but nobody bothered him. The premiere had a red carpet with a big wall of sponsored logos, but that was about it. The detective guessed there were three or four photographers, a video guy, but they didn't look like the celebrity-hungry paparazzi Gregg had seen on TV.

It was a "small" picture, possibly a "dead" picture, Gregg realized, an "indie" with not a single superhero or comic-book character or a billion dollars in phony baloney CGI crap. Larry Gregg's esteem for Lowanna Xanderson suddenly went way, way up. She was coming to this premiere to support the art of filmmaking, and her eager young actor stood to one side looking shy and forlorn with his barely legal date, she in white and gold, he in a rental tux—

Probably from the same place I got this suit, Gregg mused.

The premiere now seemed honest to Gregg, even in its shabby phoniness. It would look real in *The Hollywood Reporter* and *Variety*, he figured, though it probably wouldn't even get mentioned in *The LA Times* or on *Entertainment Tonight*.

That's when Gregg spotted her—Lowanna Xanderson—scurrying out from around Starbucks, holding her heels and her purse. She'd run the six blocks to get there in time. Gregg postulated it wasn't the first time Lowanna Xanderson had scrambled through the streets barefoot for one reason or another. She was gorgeous in her gown, stunning in her commitment.

Gregg decided right then and there: Wanda was okay, but when it came to Lowanna, he was stone-cold *in love.*

Still, Gregg had a job to do, and a commitment of his own to Julie Baker and her parents, and to George Landon and to George Landon's wife—or widow, God forbid—and he intended to keep it. He angled to intercept the agent.

"Just give me a minute," Ms. Xanderson said, holding up one finger, acknowledging Gregg standing there.

The detective took pity and allowed the woman to greet her star, and shake the hands of various publicists, directors, producers, etc.—Gregg had no idea, but they seemed to be important, at least to the agent. He even allowed her to pull the principals in and get a photo for the cameras in front of the wall of brand-names, all smiling—

The detective moved in, suddenly aware that Lowanna Xanderson, now that she'd taken the "money shot," was planning to dive into the theatre, or run the other way, to evade him. He grabbed Lowanna's elbow and pulled her aside. Despite the heavy security at the event, nobody stopped him.

"Don't force me to make a scene in front of all these reporters," Gregg threatened.

Lowanna took a moment to decide.

"They'll arrest you," she told the detective. "You have no standing here. This is Hollywood and I'm as close to the Queen of Hollywood as you're going to find."

Gregg laughed a great, big roaring laugh that shook him to the core. It was infectious, and suddenly Lowanna was laughing, too, and wiping tears from her eyes, destroying her makeup but she didn't really care.

"I'm sorry," she blurted out. "That was..."

She couldn't find the word.

"Ridiculous?" Gregg suggested.

"Okay okay," Lowanna agreed. "Listen," she said when she'd sobered. "Rayna is fine, just fine. But I can't let you talk to her. I can't force her to contact her parents. I'm in a precarious negotiating position right here. Her whole career is at stake."

"I need to know more than that," Gregg insisted, getting serious now.

"I know, I know," Lowanna answered. She looked up at Gregg, who was easily a foot taller with her heels off. Maybe she liked him or maybe she just took pity on him—Gregg didn't know—but he suddenly trusted her, and understood she would be straight with her. She reached into her handbag—

Gregg tensed, ready to disarm the bitch if she went for a weapon—

"Here's my card," Lowanna said, taking out a gold engraved card, elegant and rare-looking—a museum piece. "That's my cell. For you only—you give that out, I'll kill you. Call me after ten a.m. tomorrow morning. We'll meet for lunch near my office—nothing fancy, casual attire—and I will tell you the truth, I swear. I only want what's best for my actors, that's all."

She put her heels back on, checked herself, took out a mirror and tweaked her makeup.

Gregg watched.

Yeah, definitely in love.

"Tomorrow lunch," he said, a stunned, love-struck pre-teen boy with his first boner—unexpected, painful, and full of promise. "Will Rayna be there?"

"No, but I'll talk to her before that. I'll tell her to call home."

"She do everything you tell her to do?"

"No," Lowanna admitted, "but if I explain, maybe she'll talk to Dear Old Mom and Dad and tell 'em to call off the dogs—"

"Me."

"Yeah."

"I'm the dog?"

"You're a puppy," Lowanna Xanderson smiled, reaching up and petting Larry Gregg's cheek. If she'd asked him to beg, or roll over, or fetch or sit, he would have done it right then and there, in front of them all, on the off-chance she'd rub his furry little canine tummy.

"What about my partner? What about George Landon? What happened to him?" Gregg asked, turning his desire to anger.

"Honestly, I have no idea what you're talking about," Lowanna Xanderson told Gregg, and he believed her.

She scurried away. Gregg was tempted to chase after her, maybe even see if he couldn't catch the film, too, for free—he'd never seen a movie for free in his entire life. Everybody here did that, he noticed. The studios *begged* people to come see their films if they belonged to a guild or the Motion Picture Academy, or voted in the last election, or were otherwise important.

But Lowanna Xanderson was already stopping to have more photos taken. Gregg wondered if she'd even make it inside to catch the flick. He wondered if that even mattered. He wondered if he should offer to drive her back when it was over. He *was* her chauffeur, after all.

As the cameras angled around, Gregg realized it wouldn't do to have his picture in the news, even if it was only a trade-paper, even if he was only in the background.

Not the way a good detective stays under the radar, Gregg decided. Besides, his phone was ringing.

It was the Los Angeles Police Department, Missing Persons:

"We found your colleague's car, the Chrysler."

"Are you sure?" Gregg asked, catching his breath.

"Positive. George Landon, registered owner."

"Where? What? Fill me in," Gregg begged.

"Found abandoned in West LA, impounded to an impound lot in Venice."

"Was...my colleague?" Gregg started to ask.

"No, he wasn't in the trunk if that's what you were going to ask," the detective said. "Not much of anything in there. Plates had been taken. We tracked it to Landon with the VIN number."

"Have you done prints, forensics?" Gregg asked.

"Nah, not yet," the detective said. "This is the first we got wind of the car being of any interest. But we will. Tomorrow."

"Tomorrow?" Gregg started to protest.

"The lot's closed now—just guard dogs."

Gregg didn't press the point. The man had gone out of his way to help. Besides, Gregg had a different favor to ask.

"I want to be there," Gregg said.

"That's pretty irregular."

"He was my partner. My buddy," Gregg argued.

"Well, okay," the detective reneged. He gave the Minnesota detective the time—10 am—and place—Boofy's Tow on Glencoe—and hinted that the only reason he was doing that was because the detective assigned to the case, a Detective Jamison, "was an LAPD officer, but not exactly 'LA's finest,' if you know what I mean. Maybe you'll see something he misses."

"Okay, I'll be there," Gregg answered.

It was fully dark by then. With a couple of hours to kill while Lowanna was in the movie—he'd decided to drive her home if she'd let him—there wasn't much else for Larry Gregg to do but drive back to Hollywood and wait around across from the building where Jack C. Cunningham lived. Gregg had no idea if his target had gone out earlier or was inside; all Gregg could do was wait. It was warm here, at least, as compared to Minnesota, even at night, though not *that* warm, and Gregg felt for the homeless men, women, and children who were scattered through the area, finding what little shelter they could. Unlike other detectives who despised stakeouts and the long, boring hours, Gregg enjoyed the solitude and the time to think. He gazed down the street, empty of traffic this time of an evening, cars parked impossibly close to each other, bumper to bumper, not a spare spot in sight—

Gregg froze. Something about a Subaru caught his attention.

What is it about that car?

Gregg quickly realized it was the license plate—from his home state of Minnesota. "Explore Minnesota. 10,000 lakes." *That's the best slogan they could come up with?*

But that's not it...it's the number...but that's not George's car.

Gregg froze. He stood straight. The car was a half-block down, an average-looking Subaru-something, dirty but not mud-caked. The windshield was clean, however—it wasn't abandoned.

But those plates...

Gregg pulled out his phone and hit a number on speed-dial. The phone picked up before the first ring finished—

"Larry!" George Landon's wife almost shouted at the other end. "What? Tell me. Make it quick."

"I haven't found him," Gregg said quickly. "Not yet, but I will."

"Thank God," the woman sighed at the other end. She had expected the worst. It was later where she was—two hours later than LA.

"But I need your help," Gregg told her. "George's car—he's still driving that Chrysler, right?"

"Yes, of course."

"He wouldn't have traded it in on a Subaru, would he?"

"No..."

"You know the license number?"

"No, I...it's some weird number and letters. George never went in for those fancy vanity plates—"

"You have your insurance card in your wallet?" Gregg asked.

"Sure—"

"That's got the license number."

"Hold on a second..."

Gregg waited. He had a horrible feeling about this. He was having a lot of horrible feelings lately. He didn't believe in ghosts, he didn't believe in the supernatural, nor did he believe in ESP, but he believed in a cop's gut, and his was giving him fits ever since he arrived in Tinsel Town.

"I have it here," George Landon's wife said at the other end of the phone.

Gregg took a few steps toward the car in question. Daylight was gone but he could still make out the numbers—

Landon's wife read the letters and numbers slowly over the phone—an exact match.

"That's uh..." Gregg tried to say. It was too complicated to explain now and dread had seized his throat—

"You found the car?"

"No, not exactly. I don't know what I've found. I'll call you back—"

"When?" the desperate woman on the other end of the line wanted to know.

"Ten minutes, tops," Gregg replied. "Hang in there."

Gregg hung up on his best friend's wife, hoping she'd forgive him. This was one of those "cover your own face with the oxygen mask first, then help the other person" sort of situations as far as Gregg was concerned. He turned his phone off. He didn't want Rachel Landon calling in the middle of this particular task. He wasn't sure his heart could stand that.

Gregg approached the vehicle. It wasn't the kind of Subaru with a hatchback, and it wasn't a station wagon, which dismayed Gregg—he couldn't just look in back, he'd have to pop the trunk. He took out his keys, which were attached to a small, novelty flashlight, which he used to peek in the back seat. Nothing unusual. The owner was no better at housekeeping on the interior than the filthy exterior. Gregg could see candy wrappers, receipts, wadded-up papers. Whoever owned this had left evidence, at least. Gregg took the long way around the car, sniffing the air, hoping not to detect any foul odors, the kind released by dead bodies. Relieved, smelling nothing, he walked back to his own car and retrieved his Slim Jim. Using the device, he popped the Subaru open and pulled the lever for the trunk. The lid jumped only an inch or two. Gregg paused. He'd have to lift that lid himself. He still smelled nothing, which gave him courage. He turned on his flashlight again and jerked the trunk-lid into the air the way you'd pull off a band-aid, pain all at once, quick and over.

Gregg gasped at the sight of his friend and partner, George Landon, dead, wrapped in a light rain-jacket, his big body curled up small into a fetal position, face crushed against the front wall of the small space, eyes open in terror. There was no point in touching him. All Gregg could do was stare, and try not to scream or cry or hit something hard. There'd be time to investigate later—for starters, someone had poured some kind of powder all over him—lime, Gregg guessed, the kind from the garden store. Whoever did this probably unknowingly meant to dissolve the body. Gregg knew that wouldn't work. It did hide the odor, however, and even now—Gregg could tell that his friend was a week or two dead—there was no smell of rotting flesh.

Gregg tried to think what to do. He should call the cops first. Or Landon's wife. *Which?*

A clunking sound was the last thing Larry Gregg heard in his life. Something to do with the back of his head. Someone had either hit him hard with a blunt instrument—baseball bat or iron bar, possibly a two-by-four—or he'd just suffered a massive stroke. Either way, Larry Gregg's last thought alive was that he was dead meat and for once in his life he was right.

Now it didn't matter who he called first. He'd call neither.

CHAPTER 25

Okay, I'm in deep *Pulp Fiction* (1994) shit right now, bordering on a Christopher Nolan breakdown. My head's going all *Matrix* (1999) on me, with a strong *Memento* (2000) component. I don't know what's happened in the past, or what's going on right now. The future seems like it's behind me, tapping on my shoulder, and if I turn around it's going to be Jason or Leatherface or Freddy Krueger with a knife or a chainsaw standing there—

I checked the perimeter of my apartment again. I call it an apartment but it's one fucking room, let's face it, with a john and a stove and a huge freezer (I got a deal) and a refrigerator. I know, I know, loser talk, which I counsel against. Breathe, damn you, breathe.

I'd mentioned Nathanael West's *The Day of the Locust* to a woman I'd hooked up with the night before off the internet and how a character in the book had come to Hollywood to make it big and had lost an arm, then a leg, then the other arm until he'd been whittled down to nothing—

"*A Cool Million*," the woman interrupted.

"What?" I asked.

"The book you're thinking of is Nathanael West's *A Cool Million*," she said, "not *The Day of the Locust*."

I stared. Here was a cheap, needy, wannabe-but-never-will-be "actress" trading literary allusions with me—

"No biggie," she shrugged.

She laid back in my own goddamn bed, tits perky and bright the night before, now sagged into her body, the bitch, a werewitch certainly, shape-shifter, telling *me* what the fuck I'd read—

She wasn't that heavy and her bones didn't weigh much. I had her in the plastic containers and the new freezer by noon and most of her bones up in the roof-top water-tank with Elena Mejia and the others by early evening.

All was fine in the tank. There was no smell, but not much decomposition, either. It didn't matter. I'd be gone soon, I figured. I was becoming impatient. I had plans. In the next month I'd either be rich or I'd be dead.

CHAPTER 26

Detective Hack Jamison fumed. He was supposed to meet some podunk hillbilly private dick from Mooseshit, Minnesota, at the impound lot, and the rube hadn't even shown.

I don't need this, Jamison told himself. He'd just discovered close to ten million dollars in exotic stolen vehicles, in three different warehouses, a literal Pebble Beach Concourse in Santa Clarita—"a bigger collection than Jay *fucking* Leno's," the supervisor had declared. Jamison had made the mistake of calling it in, stepping back as he'd been instructed, while a swarm of other detectives swooped in to take VIN numbers, dust for prints, look up the cars on the lists of stolen vehicles.

"Get lost," they told Jamison. "We don't want you screwing this case up."

Now he was back in Venice, or Marina Del Rey—he didn't know where the hell he was, waiting for a ghost. The phone number they gave him went nowhere. He left a message.

"Bullshit," he muttered.

That same day, a phone-call came into the Hollywood Division of LAPD:

Sgt. J. Kellogg - Dispatcher: Hello, Hollywood Division. How may I help you?

Henking: Yeah, I...uh...I think I need to speak to someone involved in that murder...

Dispatcher: What murder, sir?

Henking: The Porter Skully murder. I might have something on that. Or not. I don't know.

Dispatcher: May I have your name and location, please?

Henking: You need that?

Dispatcher: I have your name here on caller ID as Brett Henking, your location is Screen Actors Guild West, your phone number as area code 3-1-0—

Henking: Okay okay. You've got it. I work here. Membership department. It's crappy work and it pays crap but it's show-business—

Dispatcher: I'll redirect you to the detectives—

(BUZZ. MUSAK. "Theme from a Summer Place" by Percy Faith. 55 seconds.)

Detective Lt. M. Hoffsberger: Detectives. Hoffsberger. You have information on the Skully murder?

Henking: Maybe. I don't know. It's sort of just a "see something, say something" thing at this point, if you know what I mean—

Hoffsberger: Spill it, sir. Get it off your chest. You'll feel better. I'm here to listen.

Henking: Wait a minute. I didn't kill him.

Hoffsberger: Uh huh.

Henking: I work at SAG, okay? In the membership department. I field calls and make sure people are up on their dues and have their cards and are qualified to work and I help people out who are confused about the process—

Hoffsberger: Got it. I'm a member myself.

Henking: You're in the Screen Actors Guild?

Hoffsberger: Over twenty years. Bit parts—"go back to your homes," "Damn hippies!"—that sort of thing.

Henking: Anyway, I just got this call a couple of hours ago from a guy who wanted Porter Skully's name. He said he was the real Porter Skully and now he wants to use Porter Skully's name since the other one is dead.

Hoffsberger: (whistling sound signifying significance approx. 2 seconds) Hold the line, don't hang up.

(BUZZ. MUSAK. "I'm Lost Without You" by Robin Thicke. 37 seconds.)

Hoffsberger: Stay right where you are. We'll be right over.

(CLICK. END CALL.)

Ten minutes later, detectives burst into the Screen Actors Guild offices on Wilshire, commandeering the place for the next three days.

Less than a mile away, Lowanna Xanderson fumed. The night before, after the premiere, she'd gone all the way up to Izzy Clurman's house to talk to Rayna, aka Julie Baker, and had made a "scene" with Izzy and some creepy young actor who was hopped up on Human Growth Hormone, it seemed to Lowanna. Lowanna had been trying to help the detective out—Gregg was his name—who Lowanna was definitely attracted to, and not only for personal sexual purposes. She considered it her good deed for the day, and besides, he was a good-looking guy with a certain "Xanderson factor," which meant he might qualify for movie super-stardom if handled just correctly, and Lowanna Xanderson knew just how to handle a man like Gregg.

But he hadn't called. She'd given him her own personal business card, a rare event generally accompanied by some ceremony and the blowing of trumpets, and now he hadn't used it as instructed. He hadn't even shown up after the screening to take her home. And now it was the next day and Rayna might already be waiting at the coffee shop for the agent and the detective to show up, so Gregg would be satisfied, make the ID, take a picture and send it to the worried parents back home, leave them alone for awhile to get back to their plans—

"The limo driver's number!" Lowanna shouted at Wanda at the front desk. "Give me the limo driver's number!"

Wanda reached for the Rolodex—some things in Hollywood never change—

"No, not *there,*" Lowanna corrected. "From the phone. Caller ID. Look it up on the internet if you have to."

Wanda did as she was told while Lowanna explained:

"The guy who drove me last night wasn't a real limo guy. He was a fake. I don't know how."

"Oh, gee, very odd," Wanda said, realizing her mistake, feigning ignorance, badly. Lowanna was reminded why Wanda had never made it as an actress. It was obvious Wanda had leaked the information— "Got it!" Wanda exclaimed.

Lowanna dialed. It was Gregg's voice all right at the other end. Wanda recognized it. She'd been thinking about him. She'd almost gotten into his pants. Next time she would.

Voicemail. Not there. "Leave a message."

Lowanna did. Smooth, nothing incriminating, but he'd get the message— It was never returned.

CHAPTER 27

It wasn't *Day of the Locust* I was living anyway; it was Horace McCoy's novel, *I Should Have Stayed Home.* In that one, in the thirties, I think, some big lug from Podunk, Georgia, comes to Hollywood 'cause this swishy producer saw him in a play in his podunk town and told him he'd give him a screentest. Instead, this guy's doing extra work (which isn't a living anymore, any more than shoe-shining or buggy-whip manufacturer). He gets hooked up with a fancy older woman who's going to make him a big star after she gets him off a few times (she figures), but he's such an idiot, he doesn't even know how to play that game, the oldest one in the book, 'cause he's such a dumb-ass virgin and all.

The similarity between that book and my life made me a little uncomfortable with the plagiarism. In our case, it was Rayna who was picked up by the horny older patron, and I was left out in the rain, even as the handsome one. In the book, the guy and his girl shared a bungalow, though they never got it on—Rayna and I didn't either, come to think of it, but we might have if we'd shared a place. I might even have insisted on it and all this crap wouldn't have happened.

It was a lot to think about as I voyeured the hell out of Izzy's mansion that night.

As soon as Izzy Clurman left I scrambled down the hill and hurried to the front door.

The maid answered.

"I need to talk to Rayna," I told her.

"No Rayna here," the maid tried, pretending not to hear, or speak English, but I knew better.

"Rayna!" I screamed into the house. The maid didn't budge. I hoped Rayna would come down and send the woman away.

"Ella no estoy aqui! Comprende?" the maid said.

"I don't believe you," I told her. I needed to work quickly. The maid's right hand wasn't visible. She might already have her finger on the alarm, the panic button, a can of mace, stun-gun, .45. I listened for sirens.

"Rayna!" I screamed again, doing Brando in *Streetcar* (1951), all weak and needy and yelling "Stella." I loathe that film. If a guy's gotta rip his shirt and get down on his knees for a woman, just 'cause he thinks he "loves" her—

"I need to speak to Rayna," I repeated, calmly now, removing my hand from the pocket of my pants, hitting the button for that powerful spring-action—

"Sí sí," the maid answered without looking at me, just the knife, which was okay by me. We all look the same to them anyway. I'd be the "handsome gringo" if she ever had anything at all to say to the police, but my guess was five hundred years of cultural conquest and white man's subjugation and possible illegal entry into the country had sewn her lips permanently and the last thing she'd be would be a snitch or a rat. Maybe I'd come back later and fuck her. She was actually quite attractive. Slap her, maybe. Spank her fat ass. Maybe we'd have a love affair. Maybe Rayna would watch and enjoy that.

Is that why Izzy hired her?

Keep your mind on the prize, I reminded myself.

Rayna came down the stairs.

I quickly put the knife away before she could see it. The maid knew where it was—that was the important thing.

"Jack?" Rayna called as she descended.

I pushed past the maid, who did not resist.

"Come up to my room," Rayna whispered. "Quickly, before Izzy gets home."

We scurried upstairs. Rayna's room was large, comfortable, and overlooked the canyon with glimpses of LA beyond, and Century City, maybe even the beach on a clear day. It really was spectacular.

I figured we had twenty minutes, half-hour tops, before Izzy showed up again with some young stud to double-team her. Maybe I'd get lucky. Maybe Rayna had changed her mind and come around and a quickie with the threat of discovery might just be the spark that oxy-acetylened our relationship together at last.

"I need your help," Rayna told me urgently the instant we were in her room.

"Anything," I assured her.

"He took my phone," she said.

"Your phone?"

That could be an emergency in this day and age I imagine, but not what I expected. If we weren't gonna screw, I figured I'd at least sneak her out of the house, make a run for it—

"Izzy took my phone," she said, "as punishment for one thing or another. He's into his 'punishments'—you wouldn't believe. The phone's in his room in the drawer by the bed. I'd get it myself but he'd kill me and the maid watches everything."

"Isn't he gonna know when he sees it's gone?" I had to ask.

"I got this other one," Rayna told me, producing another phone from down in her pants. "It looks close enough."

"Where'd you get *that?*" I asked.

"A guy who was here," she replied, looking away, nearly blushing. As much as she'd done—and I'd seen enough—she still had the decency to be embarrassed by it all. A taste of Wisconsin, Minnesota, Michigan—wherever the hell she was from.

"Why don't you just use *that* phone?" I asked her.

"It doesn't have my numbers, and I don't know what its number is and nobody can call me, like you—you've been trying to call, right?"

"Oh yeah," I lied, feeling stupid. All she had to do was look at "Missed Calls" when she got her phone back to bust me on it—

"Izzy's room is just down the hall," Rayna urged me. "I'll keep an eye out for the maid. We swap the phones in a few seconds and he'll never be the wiser. The maid might tell him about you but I'll think of something."

"Let's get out of here," I told Rayna. "Come with me. Just go. You don't have to do this."

Rayna laughed.

"You're kidding, right?"

"No, I'm not kidding."

"Izzy's going to put me in one of his movies, Jack!" she said, as if I was the dumbest guy in the whole world and what the fuck was wrong with me?

I said nothing, just snatched the phone from her hand and pointed down the hall, one eyebrow up in the form of a question.

If I ever get to use that onscreen, it'll kill, believe me. Oscar-bait.

She nodded. I went that way. I wasn't going to give a shit, not at this point in my life.

Izzy's bedroom, which I'd seen many times before, was what you'd expect—all bed and closet and giant bathroom, arranged in open space so there'd be no privacy whatsoever, which was the idea, I suppose. The picture windows looked out over still another spectacular view of the city, including the hillside I watched from at night, and the tree I'd climbed a few times to catch a better angle. To my surprise the hill looked closer from this side, and less in the dark. Looking out, it amazed me I hadn't been spotted out there. Of course, they had more interesting things to concern themselves with—

I swapped the phones just the way Rayna described it, wondering if I wasn't making a huge mistake. I wasn't wearing gloves and I'd stuck my prints all over the damn screen, Izzy's doorknob, and the dresser. It didn't take much imagination to see how Rayna or the maid or one of Izzy's studly hires, or any of Izzy's many earlier female conquests or the men he'd wronged in other ways (hundreds of possible killer suspects) might murder him and I'd be on the hook for the crime like Ida Lupino in *I Want to Live* (1958), stuck on Death Row, but it wouldn't be a clean, nifty set constructed of plywood; it would be steel, solitary confinement, dangerous cons and deadlier guards.

I did it anyway. You can't let your imagination run wild, can you? I took Rayna's phone back to her in the hall. She turned it on and entered her password, a precaution I wouldn't have suspected her of—

The phone rang.

We both jumped and yelped out something like "eek" in tiny cartoon voices.

"It's Lowanna!" Rayna enthused, looking at the caller ID. "Hello, Lowanna!" Rayna answered, turning away, indicating "private conversation."

I leaned in close to listen anyway, figuring it was my right. I'd rescued the phone, after all. It was my phone too now, I guessed, without so much as a "Thanks, Jack—you're a real prince."

Had she forgotten I was her real agent? Doesn't she realize she's two-timing me right in front of my face by talking to Lowanna like this, like a giggling school-girl?

"Did you call your parents like I asked you?" Lowanna asked sternly.

"No...I..."

"Why not?" Lowanna demanded.

"I didn't have a phone."

"You have one now. You're talking on it now."

"I just got it back," Rayna whimpered.

"You have to call your parents," Lowanna insisted.

"I don't know. Izzy won't like that."

"I don't give a rat's ass what the fucking shit Izzy Clurman likes or doesn't like. Has he put you in a picture yet?"

"Well, not yet," Rayna answered. "I just talked to you last night—"

"Did you *hear* anything I said last night? There's a private detective looking for you," Lowanna spoke quickly. "And before that there was another one."

"Why? I haven't done anything—"

"Your parents—"

So that's who they were, I realized. Her parents sent them. *How very parental of them.* It hadn't occurred to me. All sorts of things suggested themselves, but not that. I pegged them as LAPD police detectives, the simplest explanation. If they *weren't* cops—well, that just made it easier on me, I figured. "Cop killer" hadn't sat well with me anyway.

"You want me to help you or not?" Lowanna asked. "You want a career in the entertainment business or do you want to suck cock for a living, 'cause that's about all you're good for at this point."

I almost grabbed the phone and gave Lowanna Shit-hole Xanderson a piece of my mind. There was no reason to talk to my Rayna that way. What kind of self-esteem issues would this bring up? Destroying all my efforts to give Rayna the confidence—

"Izzy's back!" Rayna almost screamed.

It was true. I could hear the door, and the maid jabbering in broken English but I couldn't make out the words, only Izzy's reply.

We were still in the upstairs hall—

Rayna hung up her phone and ran back into her room, slamming it behind her, locking it, trapping me. There was no back exit, only Izzy's room—

Maybe I could jump out the window—it was only twenty feet up—

Izzy hurried up the stairs.

"How the hell do I get out of here?" I whispered sharply into the door Rayna had just locked.

Too late—

"Oh, you again," Izzy said dimly as he came up to the hall. Behind him was a big bruiser of a man, well over six foot tall, muscles and tattoos, good hair—

"I came to see Rayna—"

"And now you're leaving—"

"Maybe," I replied, pulling my knife, flicking it open.

That stopped the two of them. I knew it would.

"Rayna!" I called through the door. "Rayna, it's Jack! I'm leaving! If you want to come with me, you can!"

"Now hold on a minute," Izzy growled.

"I've got a knife and I'm ready to kill Izzy and his pet gorilla if I have to!" I spat into the door.

"You know, I never signed up for this," the big man said, backing away, stepping back down the steps backwards, like you'd go back down a ladder, which struck me as funny at the time. I laughed, which scared the hell out of Izzy. He could deal with a guy with a knife...but a *crazy* guy with a knife.

"Okay, now, you just go, okay?" Izzy said softly, backing to a side door, opening it, positioning himself behind it.

The other guy was already out the front door—I'd have to watch for him. He could be waiting in ambush.

"Okay?" Izzy repeated, noting I hadn't moved or anything. He hid even more behind the door.

"You're just going to throw that door open when I walk by," I told him, indicating I was onto his little game.

144

"No, I'm not," Izzy protested. "There's no way. You hurry by and I can't possibly get you."

"You'll try it."

"I'll be behind the door. I won't know you're there till it's too late unless you make a huge racket. Besides," Izzy added, "I'm an old man and you have a knife."

"Who knows what you got back there," I shot back. "A knife, a gun, a bazooka."

"Right, a bazooka," Izzy said, voice dripping with sarcasm.

I truly wanted to kill him right then and there. If there's one thing I hate, it's *snark*. But I was also aware that Rayna was right behind the door where I was standing, and if I'd forgotten, her voice: "Please, Jack, just go" would have reminded me. "Don't hurt him. Just go."

"You sure?" I asked.

"I'm fine. I'll call you."

I knew that was a lie because she wasn't supposed to have a phone, remember? Izzy had taken it from her. But I played along. There was no other way to play it.

"Okay, Izzy, you close that door now," I ordered.

He did as he was told.

"I'm even locking it and walking away!" he called from inside the room.

I jumped forward, a fake. Nothing. I charged past the door, which stayed closed, and down the stairs, catching a glimpse of the housekeeper in the kitchen leaned against the counter, a knife in her hand as well, and I didn't see any onions or anything, so I figured that was for me, in case I went that way instead of out the front door.

I didn't spot the stud-for-the-night as I bounded down the driveway. Fortunately for me the gate wasn't locked, and I sprinted out onto the steep drive, which slanted down to Sunset eventually.

I pocketed the knife, slowed down, and took a deep breath.

"Another exciting adventure in the life of Jack C. Cunningham!" I announced in my best movie trailer voice. The whole escape had felt like that scene in *The Way of the Gun* (2000) where Benicio del Toro and the other guy kidnap Juliette Lewis out of a doctor's office right in the middle of the day, right out from a couple of professional killers and sharpshooters, except in my case I left Rayna behind and as far as I knew Rayna wasn't at all pregnant, and when Benicio did it there was a car they stuffed the girl into and I was on foot. It's a good film if you want to check it out, especially if you think a half-hour gun-battle in a single location is a perfectly acceptable finale for a movie. I should mention here with kudos, that it's by Christopher Fucking McQuarrie, who only wrote *The Usual Fucking Suspects* (1995), believe it or shove it.

And while we're on the subject of movies, *I Want to Live* (1958) was based on a true story, and while I enjoyed the raw brutality of putting an innocent woman to death in the gas chamber, the real woman, Barbara Graham, certainly did it, along with a quartet of numbskull guys, clients of hers in the "dating for dollars" scene. They forced their way into an old woman's house in Burbank—the house is still there; you should go see it— and ended up pistol-whipping the lady, cracking her skull, suffocating her, all in an attempt to nab $100,000 they thought was there (it wasn't). The old woman died, plus they overlooked about $15,000 in jewels and other valuables right in the lady's purse, right in the closet.

Barbara and two of her accomplices were executed in the San Quentin death chamber a couple years later.

Still jazzed by the incident at Izzy's, I took in a movie right on Hollywood Boulevard, something about a superhero returning to his home to find things are a mess and he's got to avenge the death of his family or something. It's *Hamlet* with superpowers, without the doubt, and dialogue a ten-year-old could understand. I loved it. I'd love to wreak holy shit on my enemies like that—hell, I'd like to wreak holy shit on my *family*, for crying out loud.

I thought about it all the way home, and through supper, chawing down on my favorite food—you know what that is. I found a mixture 3:2:1 of Elena and Jaime and the new girl whose name I don't even know, made for a nice hash.

CHAPTER 28

LA Police Detective Michael M. Hoffsberger had never been a lucky man. He pretty much knew the stars were aligned against him from the day of his birth. His father was a small-time crook, in and out of jail, completely unsuccessful; his mother did whatever she could to keep the family together and food on the table.

Hoffsberger grew up with a brother and a sister, moving often around Torrance and Hawthorne and South Central LA. They were generally the only white faces in a sea of Hispanics and African-Americans, which had a lasting effect on young Mike. He'd been a decent football player in high school, and had aspirations to play college ball—USC was his goal, hoping for a scholarship—when his father was busted for a more serious crime—assault—than the usual B & Es, shoplifting, handling of stolen goods. The old man's five-to-ten sentence cut short the younger Hoffsberger's athletic career; he was forced to go to work at a local supermarket after school and weekends to help out at home.

Hoffsberger did manage to graduate from high school, however, and then hopped from one menial job to another, marriage, child, divorce, then ten years as a beat-cop before a chance opportunity to jump on an emergency task-force—some sort of anti-gang, anti-terrorism operation. Hoffsberger had never quite understood the whole picture, but he'd apparently been instrumental in thwarting a major catastrophe—how, he had no idea.

There had been medals and promotions and Hoffsberger was made a detective.

"Perhaps I *am* lucky, after all," he told himself.

He was wrong about that.

Another ten years went by without a single lucky thing happening to him, no matter how many lottery tickets he bought, how many dating sites he joined, or how many good deeds he did. All the positive thinking, visualization, Feng Shui and prayer in the world wasn't helping. And now he was stuck with this dead actor guy, Porter Skully.

Who I never even heard of, Hoffsberger complained to himself as he drove to SAG headquarters in his unmarked car.

Hoffsberger and his fellow detectives could see right away they were faced with an uphill battle. "Skip" Henking—the SAG office worker who dropped the dime—couldn't provide them with any more information than what he had divulged in the initial phone call. The man who called in chasing Porter Skully's name was definitely a man, and probably under the age of forty, and not a familiar voice to Henking.

"It certainly wasn't a star," he insisted. "I know all the stars. In fact, if he was a known actor of any kind, I'd have recognized the voice," Henking bragged.

He also stood firm on his statement that the caller had never given another name, only that he was Porter Skully and wanted that name back. No one currently employed at the guild remembered anyone asking for that name, nor did they know what other name the actor was given. Calls to the studios yielded no information, nor did queries to the dozen or so payroll companies normally contracted to pay cast and crew on film and television shoots. The only recent activity for "Porter Skully" was three days as a day-player on a made-for-cable movie called "Take it Away, Sam." Detectives established convincingly that the murdered actor had played the part, his last role, and nobody else.

To the detectives' dismay, the Screen Actors Guild does not record incoming calls for privacy reasons, nor does it routinely log calls. Police were able, however, to track the specific exchange Henking referred to, but the number could only be traced to a cheap burner phone purchased at a Best Buy on La Brea in West Hollywood. The phone was paid for in cash and the buyer declined the extended warranty, so there was "no name given."

"The little bastard didn't even send in the little card," Detective Hoffsberger complained aloud in the detective's room after spending half a day on the telephone with the flip-phone manufacturer.

"Criminal mastermind," quipped a fellow detective, a noted wag in the department.

Hoffsberger almost killed him.

The phone had never been used again.

Hoffsberger tried IMDB.com on the internet—no help. Neither was Google.

With 160,000 Screen Actors Guild members, it wouldn't be easy to go through all of them to find out who had made the call. Who thought they deserved the name Porter Skully, and would somebody really kill someone for that?

The LAPD did not have the budget for a full-blown investigation, so Hoffsberger was forced to keep at it on his own time.

He filed with the court for information on "change of name" requests. Intended to be a confidential procedure, Hoffsberger would need a judge's warrant and "six to eight weeks processing."

First off, half the actors were women and thus eliminated, except half of them had androgynous names like Ricki, Dakota, Dylan, Reagan, Shawn, Tanner—the list seemed endless—male or female, anybody's guess. Hoffsberger also eliminated those over sixty, who didn't live in the greater Los Angeles area, or were deceased and never dropped from the rolls. It was a monumental task, which the detective tried to further whittle down by starting with impossible names which were obvious fakes, thought up for theatrical purposes only, like Cher, Slash, Jay-Z and Raffi.

Once again, Hoffsberger was not lucky. The phone calls were heart-breaking—struggling actors answering their phones, hoping this call would be their big break, disappointed it was only the cops, suspicious at all the questions about somebody named "Porter Skully—" "Wasn't that the guy got his head cut off?" "You're selling something, right?" "How'd you get this number?"

At the end of the third batch of a hundred, after a full week had passed, Detective M. Hoffsberger was only on the "Cs" on his list.

Discouraged, Hoffsberger called his daughter, a sophomore at UCLA, drama department, having caught the acting bug as a child—endless rehearsals of *Pajama Game*, *Sound of Music*, and *Once Upon a Mattress*, along with embarrassingly age-inappropriate choices like *Gypsy* and *Carousel*, mounted by the public schools, Parks and Recreation, plus private theatre companies trying to make ends meet by bilking star-crazed stage-parents for tuition.

Nina Hoffsberger's phone didn't answer. The detective left a message. He hoped the new play was going well. He'd definitely come to a performance if she'd tell him when and where. It broke Hoffsberger's heart. He knew what it was like to be an actress; he wouldn't wish it on anybody. And it didn't make any difference if you were successful or not—he knew that, too—it was all disappointment and misery one way or another.

Like the detective business, he noted as he hung up the phone.

He went back to business, back to the "Cs" on the list. He dialed the next number listed:

"Jack C. Cunningham."

He got voice-mail, a bright, energetic young voice:

"Jack C. here, keeping it real. Out on a shoot right now, can't answer. Leave a message. You know the drill."

BEEP.

"This is Detective M. Hoffsberger of the Los Angeles Police Department," the detective told the machine. "This is not a sales call or a solicitation of any kind, and you are not being singled out as a particular target of any investigation. However, your cooperation with law enforcement is requested and greatly appreciated. Please call back."

Hoffsberger gave his number. He'd read the request off a card—there'd been meetings about exactly what to say and what not to say. Finally, his superiors had signed off on the final wording, a collaboration of a number of sources, including attorneys in the District Attorney's office.

Nobody ever called back.

"It sounds like a scam," Hoffsberger complained.

"Just read it like it is," he was told. "When they call back you can freelance then."

Exhausted, expecting nothing to come of it, Hoffsberger took the next step: he tried the internet.

Immediately, the name Jack C. Cunningham yielded a phone number in Oregon. Hoffsberger sent the number through the Federal reverse directory.

And waited.

He pictured a room full of ENIAC computers, vacuum tubes glowing red, spewing out computer punch-cards.

He felt like the jeep driver in the movie, *M*A*S*H*, who kept muttering "Goddamn Army" every couple of reels, or the cop in *The Russians are Coming! The Russians are Coming!* who kept saying "We Just Gotta Get Organized!"

Names popped up on Hoffsberger's computer monitor.

The phone number belonged to a "Jackson and Rosemary Skully."

Hoffsberger stared...

Then he leapt into the air, pumping his fists.

"You goddamn lucky sonofabitch!" he shouted, alarming the rest of the detectives in the squad room. "Lucky lucky lucky!" Hoffsberger repeated.

"Hoffsberger just got lucky," one of the wags noted.

"Yeah, wish he'd do that at home," another wit chimed in.

Hoffsberger sat again. Hands shaking, he dialed the phone. A woman answered.

"Hello, I'm looking for Porter Skully?" Hoffsberger tried.

"Oh, that's our son. He doesn't live here anymore."

"Is he an actor by any chance?" Hoffsberger asked, voice breaking. He thought he was going to cry.

"Well, yes," Rose Skully told the detective. "He is. In Hollywood."

CHAPTER 29

I'd paid for the damn thing, so I figured I should use it. It came in the mail, plain package like they'd promised. Inside was a lot of advertising offering other things, which made me think I'd just been suckered into a lifetime subscription to junk mail by ordering this.

It was one of those DNA testing kits. You had to not eat, drink, smoke or chew gum for 30 minutes before you did it, which is harder than you think—try it sometime. Then you had to put on gloves and swab inside your gums for a whole minute, which, again, is longer than you think when you're doing it, and then you have to do it again on the other cheek.

After that you just stick it in the mail and wait.

They promised there'd be a list of DNA relatives—Y-patrilineal and X-matrilineal ancestors. I had no idea what that was about—Mack and Rose weren't much on the home-schooling when it came to molecular biology (except to point out how men and plants were actually cousins and how trees and bushes and flowers control our every thought, feeling and desire, but that's another story altogether). The kit instructions did say they'd have contact information—phone numbers and e-mail and addresses and a messaging system on the internet to get hold of people who shared my DNA, or however the hell it works.

It would settle things once and for all—I wasn't related to the Skullys at all. It would help if Mack and Rose took the test, too. I considered sending a couple of kits their way. Would they just send them in on a lark? Without knowing who they were from? Or would their paranoia kick in? What if

I made them Christmas presents? Or birthday presents? HA! Better yet—
Mothers Day, Fathers Day. Or rather—"you're not my Mothers Day/you're
NOT my Fathers Day."

HA! I had to laugh.

CHAPTER 30

Rachel Landon—Detective George Landon's wife—decided to make the call, pride be damned.

"No, I haven't heard from Larry, either," Mrs. Gregg told Mrs. Landon.

"It's like they both disappeared into a great, giant black hole," Rachel Landon sighed.

"Totally," Jill Gregg agreed.

The two detectives' wives shared a moment of silence, suspecting the worst...

"Should we call Julie Baker's parents?" Rachel Landon asked, breaking the gloom.

"I..." Jill stammered. She didn't want to do it. She knew if there was any news, they would have heard. She stalled. She asked about the Landon children, a boy and a girl, one just finishing college, the other in the last year.

"They're fine," Rachel said, "and yours?"

Jill and Larry Gregg also had two children, two girls, one finishing high school, the other in her first year of college.

"Great. Can't complain," Jill told Rachel. "We're very lucky."

"Yes. Blessed," Rachel Landon agreed.

Still, the call had to be made, and as soon as the two wives hung up, Jill dialed again:

"Hello."

"Is this Julie Baker's house?" Jill asked.

"Yes," Julie's mother, Millie Baker, answered, both fear and hope in her voice.

It broke Jill's heart.

"This is Jill Gregg. I'm the wife of the detective you hired," Jill said quickly so as not to raise false hope. "The second detective."

"Oh."

"Any news on your daughter?" Jill asked.

"Not a word..." Millie confessed, holding back a sob. "How about you? Have you heard—"

"No, I haven't heard from Larry for several days and I'm starting to get worried," Jill confided.

"Like the first detective," Millie Baker stated, voice quivering.

"George Landon," Jill filled in, daring to speak the name.

"You know him, don't you?"

"Yes, he and Larry are great friends," Jill replied, careful to say "are" instead of "were."

"I am so, so sorry," Millie Baker exclaimed. "Marston and I never thought it would be this much trouble. We thought somebody could find her if she was still alive...and if not..."

She couldn't finish. Jill didn't know what to say. Anything she said would only cause pain—

"...at least we'd know she was no longer alive..." Millie Baker finished, summoning all her courage. "And now two husbands and fathers have disappeared following our daughter into...into...what? The vortex or something. I'm so, so sorry."

"It's not your fault," Jill insisted. "They're both big boys. They can take care of themselves."

"I hope you're right," Millie Baker stated forcefully. She knew in fact her Julie Baker was not a "big girl." She was certain Julie had no idea how to take care of herself, not in a big city like Los Angeles, not in a brutal industry like the motion picture business. Millie had heard stories. She'd seen things on TV, in the paper, on the covers of the magazines at the checkout at the grocery store. If a tenth of it was true...

"Julie doesn't have a chance," Millie Baker concluded, mind wandering. She knew she still held the phone in her hand...she wondered why.

"I'm going to give you a couple of numbers," Jill told the other woman. "One is mine and the other is Rachel Landon's. She's George's husband. If you hear from Julie, or either of our husbands, or the police or anyone, you give us both a call."

"Certainly. I'll do that."

"And we'll do the same," Jill assured the woman.

"Thank you."

Jill tried not to cry.

Julie Baker's mother didn't even try.

CHAPTER 31

I freaked. There was this thing on TV, one of those "real-life crime" things. The cops caught a serial rapist and murderer ten states away by uploading his genetic information—DNA—to a public database, where they got a match! There were other cases, too, where they found close relatives—brothers, sisters, mothers, fathers, aunts and uncles—catching people whose genetic junk was posted on the internet for every Tom, Dick and hairy law-enforcement bastard to see!

Did I shoot myself in the foot by taking those DNA swabs and sending them in? Would I be hoisted on my own petard? Whatever a petard is. (I looked it up—original IED, small French bomb circa 1500s or so, with a slow match for a fuse. Someday I might try to make one.)

It was too late. The thing was in the mail. I'd sent it in. I'd used my real name. It was just a matter of time now.

The bastards.

CHAPTER 32

Rayna Rourke, aka Julie Baker, sat down to write a letter to her parents. Due to a mix-up at the post office, Millie and Martin only received the letter a year after it was written, and six months after the postmark.

> Dear Mom and Dad,
>
> I'm fine. Really fine. I'm pursuing my acting career which is all I ever wanted to do. I'm taking acting classes from a coach named Freddy Weaver. The name may not mean anything to you, but here in Hollywood, he is the most famous acting teacher of them all, and there are quite a few. He says he will make me a star, and I believe him because he also said he's never said that to anybody else ever.
>
> I am so sorry I haven't called you or sent you any text messages or written you any emails. The one problem I've had is hanging onto my phone for various reasons. A very long story. I hope you haven't been too frantic. You probably have tried to call me a few times and gotten no answer.
>
> I'm fine. Really. Really fine. I just can't communicate at the moment, and it's not because I'm in jail or anything ha ha. It all stems from my dedication to my craft and the hours and energy are all going into that. It's weird here in this town. That's about all I can say.

I was in a play! It was called *Cat's Pause*, and it ran for five weeks right in the heart of Hollywood. From that I got a fantastic agent named Lowanna Xanderson. Again, you might not know the name, but here in the film business she's as famous as Emily Blunt (you probably don't know her, either). As famous as Zsa Zsa Gabor if Zsa Zsa was a talent agent.

I also have a manager, who's not so famous. His name is Jack and I really like him, as in "like like" but again, that's another whole story and I'm not sure what's going to happen with that. Probably won't be bringing him home for supper anytime soon, let's just say that ha ha.

It's strange here and I can't begin to list the many ways. It seems like every minute brings something stranger. (Or every stranger brings a new minute.) Right now I'm sitting in my own room in a house in one of the many canyons overlooking the city. The house is huge and beautiful and the view is spectacular. It has a pool and I've been swimming every day, even though the water's very cold sometimes. The house is worth $7,000,000 or something, but they don't heat the water for some reason. I say "they" but the house is owned by one person, a producer, who is keeping a very close eye on me with the aim to put me in his next film. I'm so excited and I hope it's a good one and one both of you can go see at the Megaplex. That's the dream, anyway. Everybody here is so creative and so driven to make movies, it's amazing.

Anyway, because of my situation I can't send you my phone number or my address at the moment, but I assure you I am okay and all grown up and behaving well and staying far away from any danger.

Love you very much,

Julie

Julie folded the paper, put it in an envelope and sealed it up. There were stamps in the sideboard and a tray where the outgoing mail was placed every morning for Izzy Clurman's main assistant to take down to the Post Office. Even if Izzy happened to see the letter, and open it, Julie hadn't said anything he could get angry about, she believed. He might even let the letter go out. If he asked, she'd say she'd written to her parents to avoid them worrying, so they wouldn't come looking for her, or call the police, or file a missing person's report.

Sneaking out of the house to mail the letter was out of the question. She wasn't a prisoner *exactly...*

CHAPTER 33

Somewhere in the city of Los Angeles was an aspiring actor by the name of Jack C. Cunningham or Porter Skully, but Detective Michael M. Hoffsberger was having a devil of a time locating him.

He'd tried to get a photograph of the subject out of Jackson ("Mack") and Rose Skully in Oregon, with no luck.

"We were never shutterbugs much," Mack told Hoffsberger on the phone. "I could look, but I don't ever recall seeing any pictures. You know those people you see on TV when their house burns down or there's a flood or an earthquake and they say 'the only thing I wish is that we didn't lose all our family pictures.' Well, we wouldn't be one of those," Mack confided with a glib laugh. "Instead, we'd be one of the 'I'm just glad we're all still alive' types," he added. "Or maybe 'we never thought something like that would happen around here' people—who knows what you're gonna say in a situation like that—"

"What about school pictures? A yearbook photo?" Hoffsberger interrupted.

"Home-schooled."

"Driver's license?"

"Never had one. Said it was 'government overreach'—can you believe that? Crazy kid. Where does a kid get ideas like that?"

Hoffsberger didn't know. They said good-bye and the detective searched elsewhere for a photograph of Porter Skully aka Jack C. Cunningham. He tried all the law enforcement databases—no luck. The State Department reported no passport application.

"Bigfoot's been photographed more often than this guy," Hoffsberger complained bitterly. The task of finding some sort of picture was compounded by the fact Porter Skully was also the name of the actor who got himself killed. As an actor, the other Porter Skully made sure his picture was taken as often as possible, and widely distributed.

"*Doppelgänger*," Hoffsberger muttered to himself—something he remembered from English Literature 101 in college. A required course? Hoffsberger couldn't remember, just the word and the concept: an exact copy of a person, clone, stunt-double, shadow, twin. *Dr. Jekyll and Mr. Hyde, Portrait of Dorian Grey.*

"*Doppelgänger?* I hardly *know* her," Hoffsberger joked to himself.

But a *Doppelgänger* needed to *look* like the original, and Hoffsberger had no idea what the other Porter Skully looked like.

Ignoring what Mack Skully had said, Hoffsberger checked with the Oregon Motor Vehicle Department anyway—no Porter Skully, no Jack C. Cunningham. On a hunch, suspecting that "government overreach" crap ran in the family, Hoffsberger looked up the driver's licenses for Mack and Rose Skully. To his surprise they both were duly licensed, smiling faces and all—solid citizens from what Hoffsberger could see.

The hapless detective jumped on the phone and dialed once again.

"Hello," came a young voice, a preteen.

My lucky day? Hoffsberger wondered.

"Is this the Skully residence?" the detective asked.

"Yes. You want to talk to my mother or father?"

"No, actually, I want to talk to you."

"Me?"

"Porter Skully is your older brother, isn't he?" Hoffsberger asked.

"Yes. Do you know him? Do you know where he is? When's he coming home?"

"I honestly don't know, dear, but I'm looking for him and maybe you can help me."

"How?"

"One question. Does Porter look like your mother or your father?" Hoffsberger tried.

She laughed.

"What's so funny?" the detective asked.

"He looks just like Daddy. He has a lot more hair and he's taller and skinner, and handsomer, but they look just alike. He's very handsome, don't you think? He could be a movie star—everybody says so. He's also an asshole. You tell him I said that."

Hoffsberger stared at the phone. *Asshole?* He wondered if he should pursue that—*like the kind of asshole who would slice somebody's neck open and try to steal his name?* The detective held his tongue, afraid of the answer, afraid of getting tossed from the force. *How old is this girl anyway? Whatever she said wouldn't stand up in court anyway, goddamn Constitutional law.*

"Thank you. You've been very helpful," Hoffsberger told the girl. "What's your name?"

"Lilly."

Hoffsberger wrote the name on his note-pad.

"Good-bye, Lilly, and thanks again."

The detective hung up. He hurried to print a copy of Mack Skully's picture from his driver's license.

When that proved to be useless—"like this guy only twenty years younger"—a week later, out of frustration, Hoffsberger asked the local police in Oregon to send a sketch-artist out to the Skully compound, where the whole family gathered to describe Jack as best they could.

"A real cluster-fuck," the sketch-artist complained. "You ever try to draw something by committee? It's like none of these people had ever seen him, they had so many different ideas. Remember Confucius? 'Man with two watches never knows correct time?' Well, multiply that by the whole clan—it's a miracle I didn't blow my stack and murder them all."

Hoffsberger received the drawing the next day. He compared it with the driver's license picture of Mack Skully. They didn't look at all alike.

"Lilly Lilly Lilly," Hoffsberger complained, shaking his head. Lilly had either lied to him or she was blind as a bat. "Either way, pathetic," the detective noted.

Immediately, he got on the phone to the local police in Oregon and requested DNA samples from the entire family.

"You got a warrant?" Oregon wanted to know.

"Ask them nicely," Hoffsberger suggested.

"We'll give it a try," they told him.

CHAPTER 34

I was torn, of course. Izzy Clurman might still be of use to Rayna and me. It was the only reason he kept breathing.

Lowanna Xanderson was another story, however. She was flat-out in my way, and not just *my* way, *our* way—me and Rayna.

What I didn't tell you—I had Lowanna's phone number all along. I took it off Rayna that night in the coffee shop when she wasn't looking. She went to the john and left her purse—why do girls do that? It was a nice purse—maybe she didn't want to put it on a filthy bathroom floor? I took the phone out—that's all I cared about. I wrote down the number for "Low," and a few other numbers I was worried about, then slipped the phone back in her purse. Nobody noticed.

In a pinch, if I was desperate for money, I could probably sell the famous agent's number for bow-coo bucks on the streets, or to my acting-class buddies at Freddy's Acting Studio.

But now I had bigger fish to fry. Takin' Care of Business, Stay Ahead of Yourself. T-C-B, S-A-Y! I sang it to myself the way Aretha did in R-E-S-P-E-C-T. And dialed the phone. It was time to use that number and take care of the Lowanna Xanderson situation.

"Hello," the assistant answered. Didn't even give her name, the name of the agency, nothing—*so* cool.

"Yes, please, I hope you can help me." I put on a British accent—slightly Caribbean, Bahamas maybe, not Jamaican, not Haitian. "I'm Ms.

Xanderson's driver tonight for the premiere and I'm afraid I've misplaced the vital information. Would you please...?"

"Is this Larry?" the woman whispered.

Who the hell is Larry?

"Uh, no..." I answered.

"Larry Gregg, the detective? Cut the crap and the accent. It's me, Wanda. Don't tell me you don't remember me."

"How could I forget?" I answered, switching to something Middle European, Alsace-Lorraine, like Max Von Sydow in *Three Days of the Condor* (1975).

She wasn't buying it, I could tell. Nothing worse than a woman's thorough disgust, and I felt it right then, through the telephone wires, over to the cell tower, up to the satellite and back down to my scorched ear. The little bitch (and I don't use that term lightly) assured me they would find a different limo service in the future, despite my apologies and explanations, and she "didn't give a flying fuck" if I got fired or not—

"Could I have Lowanna's cell number as well?" I asked. "In case there's any problem."

"Fuck you," she answered matter-of-factly, disguising her rage, and hung up.

"No, fuck *you*," I answered to no one in my own voice, the picture of politeness. I hung up. There had to be some other way. E-T-O-P—Eyes on the Prize. D-G-I-F—Don't Give in to Fear.

───────◆◆───────

In the office, Wanda stuck her tongue out at the phone.

"Who was that?" Lowanna Xanderson asked. She'd come out of her office. Wanda hadn't noticed.

"Who was what?" Wanda stalled—*how long had Low been standing there?*

"The caller you just said 'fuck you' to."

"Oh, nobody, just another joker trying to get your address and phone by pretending to be a limo driver—"

"Call him back! Right now! I want to talk to him—"

"It's not who you think it is," Wanda warned. "It's not the detective—"

"Now! Immediately!" Lowanna ordered.

Bitterly, Wanda checked the number of the last caller. The last thing she wanted to do was dial it. She wrote it down, knocked on Lowanna's door and gave it to her boss.

"Thank you," Lowanna answered flatly.

I couldn't believe it. Lowanna Xanderson was calling me! I cleared my throat, let it ring another time, then picked up.

"Yes?" I answered with the Caribbean accent, a last-minute choice.

"This is Lowanna. Pick me up at my house at seven."

"I'll need the address," I told her.

She gave it to me. Emboldened, I pressed her for her cell-phone number, too.

"Yeah, you better have it," she admitted. "We'll talk when you pick me up, and in the car. The screening's in Santa Monica—we'll have time."

"Excellent," I told her.

"And lose the accent—it really is terrible," she told me right before she hung up.

"Whatever you want," I said to the phone in my own voice, but with a sinister quality—Clint Eastwood in *Dirty Harry*, Peter Lorre in *The Maltese Falcon*.

I spent the afternoon lining up a limousine, suit and hat—rentals all. You can rent anything in Hollywood, including Alpaca's. I googled the hell out of everything and figured out how to get to "Low's" ten minutes early, no more, by pulling into a cul-de-sac not too far from her place up in the canyons. I got there an hour early. I couldn't take the chance of getting lost. Those canyons are murder, and if you happen to go up the wrong road, you can really get stuck so you have to go all the way back down to Sunset just to get over to the right one and it can take hours or so, and this was one appointment I didn't want to miss.

Once in place just a few blocks from her house, I was fine. It was a private road, really, only two houses above it. I was a limo driver taking a break, waiting to pick up the next fare, wouldn't be much noticed. Hiding in plain sight, *The Purloined Letter*, invisible to the naked eye. The spot held an additional advantage—I could see the road below from there, all the way to Lowanna Xanderson's house, and if another limo pulled up—say, the real one—I'd be able to spot it. This was my one chance and I needed to seize it no matter what.

I checked my knife, opening and closing it several times. It needed a little oil; I'd take care of that later. Check the internet; see what people recommended. You can find out about anything on the internet. Somebody had probably done a YouTube tutorial. I should probably do one myself on preparing human flesh, ha ha—

But right then I needed to figure out my plan of attack. P-E-A-C-E— Pause, Exhale, Acknowledge, Choose and Engage. Later, after I'd spit-balled some scenarios, done a few mind-actualizations, played a few war-games in my head for the night to come, there would even be time for a little meditation. It was that time of year and sunset was fast approaching. It really was beautiful up there—the view was probably worth the millions it cost for a house.

———————

Lowanna Xanderson was putting on the finishing touches to her hair and makeup in the hall mirror when she heard the limo pull up. In spite of her age and station in life—one of the most powerful people in Hollywood, confirmed every year in special issues of *The Hollywood Reporter* and *Variety*—her heart went positively aflutter at the prospect of seeing the detective again.

He was her puppy-dog, the man who'd chased her barefoot through the streets of Westwood, a scene she'd relived over and over in her mind, which only became more erotic on each reimagining, ending in a hundred different scenarios, all ending with him taking her, or her taking him—

Lowanna took a deep breath and smiled at herself in the mirror. She'd try to give him a little space, not devour him on sight. Would she get in the limo in the front seat, an unbelievable violation of protocol, or would she whisper, "May I sit with you in front, driver?"

She'd already decided she'd call him "driver." She remembered his name—Larry Gregg—but that wasn't any fun.

Too sharp, too hard—

Lowanna giggled.

A horn honk brought her back to reality. He was being rude. Or maybe he was full of anticipation too. Whatever happened, she couldn't miss the premiere. She kicked herself; she could have had him come an hour earlier, inviting him in. There was never enough time—

Another horn honk.

"Coming! I'm coming!" Lowanna almost screamed.

She stepped out the front door and turned to lock it—

It was a double-take—

The man getting out of the limo, the driver, ill-fitting suit, hat and all—a chauffeur—was not the man she expected. He was handsome, all right, but too young, unweathered—not Larry Gregg, not the man of her fantasies.

Lowanna scrambled back inside and locked the door, unsure what to do. She peeked out the window next to the door.

The driver stood by the vehicle. He opened the rear door.

Lowanna fumbled with her phone. She dialed. He answered. She saw him with the phone.

"Yes?"

"Who are you?" Lowanna demanded.

"I'm your limo driver," the man said in that quasi-Jamaican accent Lowanna had so despised the first time. Of course she'd made a mistake—her beloved Larry Gregg would never do something that tacky.

"No, you're not!" Lowanna growled. "You're an imposter!"

"I'm here to take you to the premiere," the driver insisted.

"No, you're not. You're all wrong. I'm calling the police."

Lowanna showed him the phone through the window next to the door. In an elaborate, exaggerated mime, she dialed 9-1-1.

"Yeah, okay," Jack said, shutting the limo door again. "So long, bitch."

He got back into the limo and drove off.

Lowanna, shaking, ran upstairs and locked herself in her room.

"No premiere tonight," she told herself.

CHAPTER 35

Acting coach Freddy Weaver had some tweaks of his own when it came to Jack's police sketch.

"His ears are a little bigger than this and they stick out a little more," Freddy told Detective Hoffsberger. "Not Dumbo, really, but just a touch—endearing, really. And the eyebrows are a little higher up and thicker. More innocent-looking and less sinister."

After a dozen other criticisms, just when the detective was about to cut the acting teacher off, or suggest maybe he'd like to sit down with the sketch artist, Freddy suggested: "Why don't you just get a copy of his eight-by-ten glossy?"

"Do you have one?" Hoffsberger asked eagerly.

"No, not me, but I know he had one done. I saw it. Not bad, really. I referred Jack to the photographer—"

"Who?" Hoffsberger wanted to know.

"Craig Ness, some side street off Sunset. Ivar, I think. 'Craig Ness Photography'—you can look him up. He still advertises in Backstage West, I think, if all else fails. Ness did me a favor once, and he's quite good, so I recommend my students to him if they ask."

"How much does he give you for that?" Hoffsberger asked.

"Me? Nothing. That would be like a 'kickback' or something wouldn't it?" Freddy asked, lip curled on one side. "Nice idea and I can always use the money, but I don't do that sort of thing."

"Uh huh," Hoffsberger commented.

"It's illegal, isn't it?" Freddy asked with unconvincing innocence.

His students were just filing in; Hoffsberger hurried out, wishing he could take a shower. He drove down to Ivar, a forgotten but charming little street running parallel to Cahuenga between Sunset and Franklin and the freeway, only a few blocks, constantly changing, with new businesses going in, old ones going bust. Hoffsberger wondered if they still had the Farmer's Market there on Sunday mornings—they blocked off the street and sold vegetables and other stuff—Huell Howser did a piece on it once, the detective remembered. Hoffsberger missed Howser—

"So does all of California," the detective muttered. "A crying shame—"

Sure enough, as Freddy Weaver had promised, a small storefront appeared with the name "Craig Ness Photography" stenciled neatly on the glass door in front. Hoffsberger double-parked and went over to the place. He tried the door—locked. He shaded his eyes and looked inside—dark. The detective checked the business hours on the door—late by a half-hour—*out of luck*. Hoffsberger started to leave when he spied a display of head-shots in the front window—product samples. He checked out the men, even taking out the police sketch to compare.

On the one hand, *none* of the young men looked like the drawing— they were all too young for one thing—but in another way, they *all* looked like it. There was a certain sameness Hoffsberger didn't understand. He looked at all the names imprinted under the photographs—none of them Jack Cunningham or Porter Skully.

As the detective got back into his vehicle, he heard police sirens heading down Sunset, going west. He followed them a while, taking advantage of them clearing traffic, but when they jogged north up Benedict Canyon Road, he let them go; he didn't need that aggravation. It was past 7:30 by then; maybe the 405 to the 118 to his home in Simi would be almost civilized.

CHAPTER 36

I couldn't believe she really called the cops on me. The sirens came up almost immediately, winding up the canyon. There was no place to turn and no place to park. In a minute I was going to face a dozen black-and-whites, and as glib as I am, and intelligent, and crafty, and a master of disguise, they weren't going to believe handsome Jack C. Cunningham was a lowly chauffeur. And then there was the name Porter Skully on my driver's license and the rental agreement and a credit card, which might lead them to investigate other avenues—

A long stretch of straight road presented itself before me, with no cars parked tight against the curb, a rare sighting in this section of the canyon. I pulled the limo over and cut the lights nano-seconds before the cops showed up—lights and sirens—roaring past without noticing me ducked down behind the dash. There would be more, I figured, and my best play was to ditch the limo and high-tail it on foot, put as much distance as I could between Lowanna, the car, and myself.

Right away I could see I'd be in for a hike. Sunset was a long ways down and Izzy's—that's where I considered going—was two canyons over with a hundred multi-million dollar estates between him and me.

So I chilled and ambled downhill. I'd come up with some other plan—

I ducked behind some cars as other police vehicles charged up the canyon. That was no surprise. Lowanna Xanderson was a top talent agent in Hollywood, maybe *the* top talent agent in Hollywood. The police came in droves, eager to rescue her. Promotions were to be made, citations, even an invite to an awards show perhaps—God be praised!—even the Oscars. Maybe even a small role in a film (as a cop), possibly leading to other things—

They're giddy thinking about it, I told myself bitterly, tossing my chauffeur's hat away over a nicely stained redwood fence, behind which I heard a snarling Doberman or German Shepherd tear the thing to pieces like a Nazi prison guard—

Mercedes in the drive: check.

I looked at my watch. By the time I would get into town, Freddy's class would be over. So maybe I'd go over afterwards. Take care of that. Or Clyde What's-his-name. Things were looking up.

I'd worry about the limo tomorrow, and the deposit on the rental hat...

CHAPTER 37

That morning, besides what he usually gave Rayna in the morning—"Hard and fast, baby—you know you love it!" (she didn't)—Izzy also handed her a script, which made Rayna's heart soar.

"Take it easy, kid," Izzy said. "It's not that great a project and it ain't a big part either."

Rayna grabbed the artifact, anxious to open it up and read it, or more likely devour it—her first real movie role, maybe.

"*Which* part?" she asked.

"Ruthie," Izzy told her. "Shows up halfway through the picture. Small part. Three lines. One day of work, but that'll get you a SAG card."

Rayna rushed Izzy, throwing her arms around his neck, kissing him over and over on his cheeks, embarrassing him.

"Cut it out," he said eventually, prying her arms away. Izzy wasn't a nice person, and he didn't like being thought of as a nice person, not even by the young, luscious woman he was fucking every night and most mornings—"Hard and fast, baby—"

"When do I audition?" Rayna asked.

"Done and done. I told the director you got the part. I'm the producer so he said 'sure.' That's the way it works, kiddo."

"Thank you, Izzy," Rayna whispered as she fell away from him, tears of joy streaming down his face.

"I gotta get to work," he said, hurrying out the door.

"I'll be here when you get home!" Rayna called after him.

As soon as Izzy's car cleared the driveway, Rayna's impulse was to grab her phone to call her parents and tell them the news.

Better not, she told herself. Izzy didn't know she had her phone back for one thing. He didn't want her calling home for some reason, any more than he wanted her leaving the house.

"I want you all to myself," he told her.

It also occurred to her, based on Izzy's varied interests in the interpersonal realm, this might not be the kind of movie her parents would want to go see at the Megaplex.

Awkward, Rayna worried.

She spent the rest of the morning reading the script. It started out okay enough: an aspiring actress, singer, part-time hooker by the name of Leslie hooks up with a mob-boss one night and inadvertently witnesses a gangland hit, which the cops just barely miss seeing themselves, so the police squeeze the woman by arresting her on another charge and in cahoots with the DA get her thrown in the clink where she's raped by a couple of really hot homosexual women (tastefully but graphically described) in the communal shower—lots of soap and lather.

The most enthusiastic woman raping the heroine, Leslie, was named "Ruthie" in the script, which made Rayna's heart sink like that ship in *Titanic* when she read it. It was clear from the little asterisks on the edge of the page and the way the scene was written in a slightly different typeface—Courier Screenplay rather than Courier Final Draft—that the scene was an add-on, stuck in later, an extra splash of T and A to whet the whistle of the ratings board and get the hard R.

It wasn't lost on Rayna that it was *her* Ts and her A described in the text, or that the scene itself was a very close approximation of a scene she and Izzy had watched together, part of an erotic compilation on DVD, one of many she and Izzy had shared viewing. Rayna understood and was sympathetic to the fact that as an older man, Izzy sometimes needed additional stimulation, and that three women together was something that aroused him. Nevertheless, she had refused to recreate the scene in real life, putting her foot down, insisting that the extra *guys* he brought home would have to do. But here it was again, essentially the same scene, with a few embellishments, and if Rayna wanted to play Ruthie and jump-start her career, with Izzy no doubt on the set watching—"just dropped in to see how it's going"—she'd have to do it all and pretend—

She charged into the bathroom and threw up, over and over, until the back of her throat scratched like a cat's claws and her head ached like a heartsick orphan child. She fell back on the cold, faux-Italian tiles, holding fast to the toilet.

"Okay," Rayna told herself, "there are no small parts, only small actors." She wouldn't be small. She would do the part, and do it well. She'd be the greatest actor she could be that day and she'd also turn Izzy on like nobody's business and get her Screen Actors Guild card to boot. So what if that's what it was all about? Who knew what was what and who cared?

As long as you get what you want, Rayna reminded herself.

CHAPTER 38

Hoffsberger woke up early and drove into Hollywood. "Craig Ness Photography" was open as promised. Hoffsberger walked right in.

An old-school smell of ink and photo chemicals assaulted the detective's nose. A couple of cycloramas were set up ready to go, with a few umbrella lights pointed at them. C-stands and apple boxes completed the decor—"Hollywood set"—unchanged since the 1920s.

A young man came in from the back wearing a leather apron, also old-school, straight from Western Costume, like a tanner at the tannery, a scowl on his face, a pair of readers dangling precariously at the end of his nose.

Nice touch, Hoffsberger noted.

"You Craig Ness?" the detective asked.

"Who wants to know?" the young man answered.

"LAPD," Hoffsberger told him, flashing his badge.

"Is that right?" Ness answered.

"That's right, and don't get smart," the detective warned.

"Can't arrest a guy for asking a question—like how come you cops just flash the badge and don't let a guy read it?"

"You wanna read, go to the library."

"I might just do that, instead of wastin' my time—"

"You know an actor named Porter Skully?" Hoffsberger asked.

"The guy who got..."

Ness made choking sounds and drew a line across his throat.

Hoffsberger mentally kicked himself—he'd used the wrong name. To everybody but him, that was the dead actor.

Need that extra cup of coffee, the detective complained to himself, the only man who'd listen. *Goddamn health kick.*

"No, hang on," Hoffsberger backtracked, correcting. "Not him. Cunningham. Jack C. Cunningham. You know him?"

"Maybe, maybe not."

"Got his picture taken here is what I heard."

"Could be," Ness shrugged. "Lots of people get their picture taken. It's a 'thing.'"

The detective smiled. He enjoyed the banter. He liked being back in the 30s, a hard-boiled detective novel, "sharp" dialogue, a couple of "Joe's" trading banter, but he had a job to do, and even if Ivar wasn't exactly a "mean street—"

"How 'bout I run you in and pistol-whip you to within an inch of your life, punk?" Hoffsberger asked, pulling his Glock. It wasn't a .38 Police Special, but the result would be the same.

"Oh, guns. Nice," Ness stated sarcastically. "Put it away. I'll give you what you want."

Hoffsberger put his weapon away. Ness looked through his files and came up with an 8 by 10 glossy.

"Here we go," Ness said. "This is the guy."

Ness handed over the photo. The man in the picture, clearly labeled Jack C. Cunningham, looked nothing like the ID photo of Mack Skully, nor anything like the composite sketch.

"Figures," Hoffsberger muttered.

"Anything else?" Ness asked. "Something for the missus?"

The detective ignored the wisecrack. That was over. He was tired of it now. He turned the photo over. A blank white sheet.

"Where's the rest of it?" Hoffsberger asked.

"That's it," Ness replied, checking the work-order that came with the photo. "He didn't want the 'resume/contact info' on the back."

"Why not?"

Ness shrugged.

"Actors move around, change their phones and addresses, get more parts they want to add to their resumes. It's easier and cheaper for them just to print out a new sheet and staple it to the back. Saves 'em a couple smackers off the Deluxe Package."

"You have contact information for this Jack C. Cunningham, right?" the detective asked, sounding a little desperate.

Ness was already shaking his head.

"Paid cash, no information. I printed out a hundred four months ago and he hasn't been back for more."

Hoffsberger reached into his suit-coat and pulled out a business card. He gave it to the photographer.

"If he comes back, you call me. Pronto. You understand?"

Ness nodded.

"What did this guy do, anyway?"

"Just call me, right away, and if I don't answer dial 9-1-1."

"And say what?"

"Say there's somebody in your shop wanted for murder," Hoffsberger hissed.

Ness whistled back.

"He killed Porter Skully, didn't he?" Ness asked.

"Have a nice day," Hoffsberger answered. "And I'm taking this with me," he added, fluttering the 8 x 10 glossy in the air.

"You too," Ness muttered to the wind.

CHAPTER 39

Rayna sat down on the bed with the script, determined to make something good out of a bad situation—"lemons into lemonade" as her mother incessantly carped.

Stop thinking about your mother. Quit thinking about your father, too. They only bring you shame. Shame shame shame. You're better than shame—

She had three lines—that was the good news. The bad news was that they were so brutally *filthy*, they didn't fit at all into Rayna's mouth, let alone come out of it again with any sense of human decency. She tried, but it sounded stupid, and silly, then her face turned red. The short running monologue concerned the anatomy of the beautiful young movie star she'd be raping in the scene and what she'd do and how she'd do it and how much pleasure it would bring her. The character of Ruthie was like the Jim McKay of rapist lesbians, running down the play-by-play even as she herself was the main instigator.

Rayna wasn't stupid enough not to understand that people liked that sort of thing—tell you what you're going to do, do it, then crow about it afterwards—even in bed, especially Izzy, and if Rayna hadn't seen his fingerprints all over this scene from the difference in fonts, she would have seen them by now. It was a male fantasy only—there just weren't that many lesbian rapists in real life to fill a Starbucks restroom, but that didn't seem to be an issue—

In a panic, Rayna called Lowanna Xanderson's number. After all Lowanna had told her to do that, "anytime you need help, reassurance, anything, I'm there for you."

Rayna got voicemail. She left a quick "call message" and dialed again.

Jack had said the same thing about calling him anytime she needed anything. Jack would know what to do.

———————

"Hello, Rayna," I answered. "What do you know for sure."

I was stalling; she had awakened me and I wasn't anywhere half ready to speak. It was only nine in the morning and I'm a bit of a night-owl as you might have guessed—WHPH—"work hard, play hard," you know.

I hadn't killed Clyde or Freddy the night before. Instead I wasted a couple hours watching some crazy superhero movie at some ancient Hollywood movie emporium—

"Jack?" Rayna asked. "Is that you?"

As you might have guessed, my voice can go a little gravelly in the morning. Rayna didn't even know it was me. If I'd been awake, I would have goofed on her a little, made her think I was somebody else—I do that sometimes.

"Yeah, it's me," I confessed. "At your service."

"He gave me a script, Jack," she said, a little bit of excitement gurgling up from deep down in her throat, which was a bit of a turn-on, I gotta admit.

"*Who* gave you a script?" I asked. Now I *was* goofing on her—I knew exactly who she was talking about.

"Mr. Clurman, of course," she told me, all respectful and all, which made me want to gag. Remember, I'd been watching her and "Mr. Clurman..."

"Is that right?" I said, playing along.

"It's a really good part, too," Rayna said. "Not big, but important. Pivotal, I'd say. It's toward the middle and everything after that in the script sort of depends on it.

"Is that right?" I said, like I really cared and wasn't more concerned with pouring myself a glass of orange juice and getting the coffee going.

"I called Lowanna to tell her about it," Rayna said, "but she wasn't answering."

"So you called me instead," I said, a little sourly, which she picked up on.

"Don't be that way, Jack. This is a big break. This is what I've been working for."

What you've been fucking for, you mean, I almost said, but I didn't. I can fake magnanimity if I need to. Just watch me.

"Well, congratulations," I told her. "Break a leg."

"Mr. Clurman says this will get me into SAG—I hope he's right. That's something I need to talk to Lowanna about. I mean, it's a small part and I'm sure it just pays scale—I don't want to make a big deal out of the money, of course—"

"Izzy gives you everything you need, doesn't he?"

"Well, yeah…"

"He's very generous, I imagine," I went on, rubbing it in. My guess was Izzy didn't give her a dime, kept her barefoot and imprisoned, and it would likely stay that way until he sold her off to some hole-in-the-wall upstairs massage/human trafficking operation someplace on LaBrea—

"Anyway, that's something I need to go over with Lowanna, I imagine," Rayna said, "even if it's not a big deal in her world."

I didn't comment on that. The goddamn coffee was almost all gone and the orange juice was hitting my stomach all wrong and all I had to eat in the fridge besides human carcasses and a guy's tattooed arm was some goddamn frozen waffles. Rayna, who was hot enough, okay—I'll give her that—but couldn't act her way out of paper bag, was fucking going to be in some kind of real movie and here I was, not even on the radar—

"Lowanna called me to remind me to call my parents," Rayna chatted on. "Isn't that sweet?"

"Who got you your phone back, Rayna?" I almost shouted at her.

"What?"

"When sugar-boy Izzy took your phone away—who got it back for you?" I asked her again, real politely, no matter how much I was seething.

"Jack? What are you talking about?"

"I'm talking about when I came up to Izzy's house, risking life and limb—with the maid and her butcher knife—"

"Yeah, okay okay, calm down, Jack. I remember. Thank you."

"You better thank me!"

"Anyway, I called my parents and told them all about my part in the movie and boy, were they thrilled to death—"

"I'm the one who fixed you up with Izzy in the first place, don't forget," I reminded her.

"What?"

"Me. I fixed you up. Got you together. At that restaurant. I swung the deal, don't forget."

"You pimped me out, Jack," Rayna told me with a hissing sound. I couldn't believe it. That wasn't the Rayna I knew.

"What did you just say?" I hissed right back at her. I wasn't above killing my own goose, even if she was going to lay eggs of gold at some point. A guy can only take so much disrespect—

"Do you want ten percent, Jack?" Rayna asked, like that would be some sort of insult to me. *I'm an agent, a manager for crying out loud—*

"Yes, I want ten percent!" I told her.

She laughed.

I forgave her for that.

"Would you go over the lines with me?" Rayna asked.

"Now?"

"No, not now," she said. "Izzy will be home soon. Tomorrow?"

I thought about it. Maybe there was a part in it for me. Maybe I could be a "dialogue coach" or something. Better to be inside the tent than outside looking in, I always say.

"Sure, I'll run some lines with you," I told the kid.

"That would be wonderful," she said, the old Rayna back—timid, grateful, corn-fed and innocent, the Rayna/Julie Baker who was "different," who could take the film business by storm—

"In fact, I hear him coming in now," Rayna told me in a panic. "I have to go. I have to hide my phone—"

She hung up on me.

It's a good thing I'm a patient man.

----•◆•----

At her end of the line, Rayna stared at the phone with a huge grin on her face. She'd lied about Izzy—he'd be at the studio for another six hours at the minimum. She knew it was the script she'd just read that allowed her to lie, and to say what she had to Jack. Saying the X-rated lines over and over had given her the courage. She chuckled inwardly. *Thank you for that, too, Izzy.*

She was toughening up. She could handle things now she never thought she could handle.

She'd make it up to Jack. He was sweet, really, protective, possessive. Izzy could be like that, too, in a different way, even when he was sharing her with some huge stud he'd picked up on the street—

Her phone rang. The ID said "Low," her agent, Lowanna Xanderson. Rayna nearly jumped for joy.

CHAPTER 40

What Detective Hoffsberger didn't know, which is one thing *everybody* knows in Hollywood, it's that an actor's "head-shot" *never* looks anything like the actor in person.

Because of this well-known fact, circulating Jack C. Cunningham's/ aka Porter Skully's glossy 8 by 10-inch, professionally photographed and printed photo resulted in exactly zero hits within the community.

Nobody recognized him.

On a hunch, feeling lucky, Detective Hoffsberger hit the brakes at a storefront acting studio/Equity-waver theatre/Casting office on Santa Monica across from an old studio with a big sign: "WANTED: EXTRAS, ALL AGES!"

He went in and showed the picture to anybody who'd look at it, a bunch of young actors—unclear why exactly they were there in the middle of the day. A lot of shaking heads.

"I can look in the files," one of the actors suggested. "See if he's come in, at least."

"Please, anything," Hoffsberger begged.

Sure enough, the files contained the same 8 x 10 glossy Hoffsberger held in his hand. The detective turned the photo over...

"Bingo."

There it was, the Holy Grail, the missing puzzle piece, what he believed he needed to find one Jack C. Cunningham aka Porter Skully, not deceased...a resume. No address, but a phone number.

"Can I make a copy of this?" Hoffsberger asked the actor who'd given it to him.

"Take it," the young man said. "Take the original. We don't care." He laughed. The detective smiled to be polite. He suddenly had that same hollow, empty feeling he had when he was in a drug house among addicts, people who had lost all sense of reality, all hope, short-sighted, getting through the day, their affliction rubbing off on him, infecting him with despair—

"Thanks," Detective Hoffsberger said quickly, turning on his heel, scurrying out into the air, such as it was, breathing deeply. Armed with the resume now, he got back into his service car and dialed the phone number at the top.

"Out of Service."

Hoffsberger slammed his fists into the steering wheel and dialed again.

Same result.

Resigned but not giving up, the detective raced back to the squad-room to try and track down the companies listed on Jack's extensive list of credits.

The second thing everyone in show-business knows—which Detective Lieutenant Michael M. Hoffsberger soon discovered—is that the list of credits—often stapled on the back of the "head-shot"—are highly suspect, slightly bogus, downright lies.

This turned out to be the case with Jack C. Cunningham as well. He had roles in student films from schools that didn't exist, roles in *films* that didn't exist, roles as an "extra," something on YouTube, which was no longer on YouTube—

"Package, Hoffsberger," the mail guy stated flatly, tossing a thick cardboard envelope on the detective's desk.

Hoffsberger opened the package quickly. It was the DNA swabs from the mouths of the Scully family members in Oregon—

"I'll be at the lab!" Detective Hoffsberger declared to the rest of the squad room (they didn't care) as he charged out and down the hall.

By the time he reached the lab, up a floor and on the far side of the building, the detective was huffing from the exertion and excitement.

"Hoffsberger," lab technician Buster Jenks stated flatly by way of a greeting. Something about dealing with blood, saliva and other unmentionable human material had turned him crabby at some point in the distant past.

"DNA," Hoffsberger managed to get out. "Anything to do with the Porter Skully murder."

"Yeah, like what?"

"Compare and contrast, Buster," Hoffsberger told the lab tech. "Compare and contrast."

CHAPTER 41

I hurried over to Izzy's house at my usual time, early evening as the sun was just going down. After huffing up the hill into the canyon, I shimmied up my usual tree, arriving at my resting spot just ahead of Izzy pulling up and letting out a couple of spectacularly built women I'd never seen before. They were laughing and teasing each other, and teasing Izzy, too, all in good fun. Both of them had long legs, big round rears and incredible racks. Pretty, too. Who am I kidding—gorgeous.

I'd made it just in time. Ten minutes later I might have missed the show entirely.

I could see Rayna in her bedroom on the phone; she was in a panic. Clearly, she hadn't expected Izzy to be home.

"Rayna!" Izzy called from downstairs when he came in. "I've got some people I want you to meet."

"I'll be right down!" Rayna called from the bedroom. She hid the phone far under the mattress, between the mattress and the box-springs, in as close to the center as possible, beyond where the maid or Izzy would sweep their hands looking for contraband.

"Never mind!" Izzy called from downstairs. "We're coming up!"

Rayna took a deep breath. She knew what that meant. Izzy would have another man with him, and they would pull Rayna into Izzy's larger bedroom with them. There'd be music and not too many preliminaries—

"Something different this time!" Izzy announced through the door as he passed Rayna's room.

Inside, Rayna heard the giggles of the two women. A shiver ran through her. She wasn't surprised, just horrified. This wasn't what she wanted—not at all. It wasn't her "thing." Didn't Izzy understand that. It appalled her. It terrified her.

Rayna swallowed hard. She stared at the script on the bed. There'd be other scripts. She'd be in films. There'd be bigger roles and better movies and awards and all the rest. Lowanna would be proud of her.

Besides, Rayna thought, *you can handle Izzy.*

With her newfound confidence, Rayna marched from the room. She turned and walked down the hall. The two women were there, pouring themselves drinks from a bottle that had materialized from somewhere, into glasses with ice, a mystery as their origin as well, one woman on each side of Izzy's bed, sort of half on and half off the bed, revealing a lot of leg sticking out from short, girlish skirts.

As Rayna entered the room and greeted the women with a cheerful "hi," Izzy turned, pulling his jacket off, working on his tie.

"This is Lenora and this is Maggie," Izzy said, introducing the pair. "Rayna, who I told you about," Izzy said to the two women. Everybody said "hi" again—

"We're gonna do the scene—the scene from the movie!" Izzy grinned with enthusiasm.

"I thought I didn't have to audition for this," Rayna protested.

"This is not an audition, silly girl," Izzy told her. "This is *rehearsal.*"

"Izzy, no—"

"Get her, girls," Izzy told the two women, who looked at each other and smiled the way a shark looks at a snake—professional courtesy—

They stalked Rayna around the bedroom while removing their clothes—

"No, seriously. Really Izzy—"

The bigger one started reciting the lines from the script as she came ever closer—Ruthie's lines—

"Wait, that's my line!" Rayna complained, still backing away.

"I gave your part away, *Julie*," Izzy told Rayna, using her real name, her Midwestern civilian name, her "Julie, the Virgin" name—

Rayna came back with the next line in the script, hoping this really was some sort of rehearsal, but the bigger woman just kept coming, hands ready to grab anything she could from one direction while the smaller one came around the bed from the other way, reciting her lines as well, the two of them naked now, completely, describing what they were going to do to Rayna when they caught up to her—

———————

Izzy Clurman was clearly enjoying the hell out of this scenario. Even from my vantage point up a tree and off on the corner of his property, I could see him drooling at the sight of the two bull-dykes stalking my Rayna, one with a full, luscious bush I couldn't take my eyes off of, the other shaved like a baby—I couldn't help noticing—cornering Rayna in the bedroom.

The way she screamed broke my heart.

"Damn, Rayna, run!" I screamed back, but nobody could hear me. With a leap, Rayna leapt on the bed, flying at Clurman in the opposite corner, nails ready to gouge his eyes out, charging between the two women like a half-back, but they were too fast and too big and they brought her down like a couple of lionesses on a gazelle, knocking her to the bed, going for her clothes, ripping them off—

Even from where I was I could hear Rayna's scream piercing the night, a wild, horrible sound that cut me in half. Without thinking I was scrambling down the tree, dropping the last six feet, running for the house, knife in hand, open now, charging for the front door. If it was locked I was screwed. If by some miracle Izzy had left it open in his fevered hurry to fulfill his sado-lesbo fantasy, I'd kill him, painfully, and get Rayna out of there.

I went right through the door—maybe it was unlocked, maybe I broke it down—I don't remember. I was charging up the stairs, hearing the two other women howling pleasure and grunting lust through Rayna's screams of outrage, both angry and scared. My corn-fed client sounded like a gazelle who knows it's going to die. And all the while Izzy Clurman laughing, yelling, directing the scene with the most vile words, screaming himself, lines of dialogue being spoken by him, not the women now, describing her desecration.

I burst into the bedroom. There was nobody there.

Stunned, thinking it was a trap, I reached for the knife in my pocket and flipped it out—

Now Izzy screamed for real—

I whirled. He was naked in the bathroom with the women, each of whom were finger-fucking the other—my Rayna—as the hot water steamed over the trio, but not hot enough to keep six ripe nipples upright, stiff and taut as a gym-rat's hamstrings on the elliptical— You could hang your hat on 'em—

My God what a sight!

My stunned lust, momentarily engorged by the tableau before me—I gotta admit it—gave Izzy the chance to slip out of the bathroom, hands held high, making no attempt to hide his own stiff, disgusting excitement. He backed away to the corner—

"Don't kill me! Don't kill me!" he choked, eyes on the switchblade in my hand.

Deal with you later, I decided—

I pivoted, to the bathroom, where the two naked women now had Rayna even more firmly pinned against the rough Italian tile of the shower, hands on her breasts now, as well as up her slit and ass, their own pubic mounds pressed against Rayna's ridiculously white thighs. Scalding hot water blasted down on all three, ricocheting around the room, steaming. Rayna was half-crying, half-screaming, trying to fight back but it was no use. There was blood, too, from somewhere, from one of them or all of them—

The bigger girl—enormous, I realize, now that I was this close—with massive thighs, breasts, shoulders, arms—abs of steel—whooped and laughed and spanked Rayna on her soaking wet butt with a ferocity—

I stabbed her first, hard as I could, with a six-foot running head-start across the spacious bathroom—

The woman looked surprised, eyes wide, in pain, turning toward me—her face was older than I thought, betraying years her body disguised. She looked down at the knife in her side, just above the bottom rib, which I desperately tried to pull out, or twist, or do something with—

"This isn't in the script," the woman stated, confused—

Rayna turned to me like a zombie, the undead, breaking my heart—

"I didn't sign up for this—"

In the mirror, I saw Izzy make a run for it across the bedroom—

"Is this some sort of improv crap?"

I leapt back, knife coming out with the blood. I charged out of the bathroom—too late—Izzy raced from the room and tried to slam the door behind him, but I caught the door and the chase was on, down the hall, where I tackled him and sent us both careening down the stairs—

Quite by accident, or the luck of the pervert, Izzy rolled to a standing position. I jumped up to grab him when a banshee scream pierced my ear and a sharp butcher knife stuck into my shoulder—my left—and I whirled, my own knife swinging in a desperate arc, slicing across the maid's throat—the maid I had seen before, nearly cutting her head off—

She fell back but I didn't linger to see her hit the floor. I was grappling with Izzy at the door—

No match, none at all—I stabbed him once, all I had time for. The screaming upstairs was deafening. The smaller woman turned out to have the bigger voice, and the cutting of her big girlfriend enraged her. What was clearly the sound of someone's head beaten against a ceramic sink—architect's gray—shook the entire house. With the butcher knife still stuck in my shoulder, I charged upstairs to see the bigger lesbian crawling from the bathroom.

"Don't kill me," she begged. "I really thought this was an audition. I thought we were going to get parts in a movie. He said she was a big star and she was in on the deal. He told us she knew what was going to happen and approved of it. She's a method actress, he said. She needs it to seem real so she can tap into her feelings—"

I drop-kicked her face so hard, teeth ricocheted against the wall.

That's when the other one, the smaller one, with the bald beaver, roared out of the bathroom like Glenn Close in *Fatal Attraction*, or any Jason movie, arms held high, a pair of scissors in one hand, a hair dryer in the other, which she swung like a tomahawk, behind which came the scissors—

My knife was so slippery with blood I *almost* couldn't hang onto it as I sliced the hell out of her throat, chest, arms and belly, steering clear of those swinging arms. I can be pretty nimble when I need to be, when my life's at stake.

Before I knew it, they were all dead—the maid, the two actresses, Izzy. That made four. One fewer than Charlie Manson killed August 9, 1969, but hell, I didn't need no "family" to do it—*solo, baby, solo!*

I was laughing like a crazy fool and didn't even realize Rayna was standing there naked and soaking wet in the doorway of the bathroom screaming bloody murder.

Then I realized. That would have made it a perfect evening, I decided—tie Charlie at least—

Or I could just "do" her...but she was in no condition, and the fact I was covered in blood didn't help the situation any, romance-wise. Me, I don't mind blood, as you may have noticed. I even like it a little. It's honest and clean, living its bright red life out of the air, the pollution, the harsh realities of this Earth.

"Relax, Rayna," I soothed. "I'm not going to hurt you."

She didn't seem to hear me. Her squeals of terror continued, deafening, overplaying it to my mind.

Save some for opening night, lady...

I folded my knife up and threw it on Izzy's bed to show her I meant no harm. I also turned my eyes away and held up my hand against her nakedness the way I figured the young men of Bofuck, Wisconsin, or wherever the hell she was from, would do it, even though I'd been watching her screw her way through Central Casting Hollywood the last month from my perch in the tree—

"Excuse me," I said, moving past her, hands up in the air, into Izzy's bathroom, intending to clean up a little. "Excuse..." I repeated, shooing her out of the way a little so as to shut the bathroom door and get a little privacy.

The horror of that first look in the mirror nearly knocked me over. I was covered in blood, matting down my hair, soaking my clothes.

And then there was that butcher knife—the maid's knife—sticking right out of my shoulder.

That's got to go, I told myself.

The shower was still pouring hot water, steaming the room—the capacity of Izzy's system was *very* impressive. Money does buy you things, like a giant hot-water tank. Despite my pain and anguish and the excitement of the violence I'd just experienced, I wondered if Izzy's *pool* was also heated, and whether it was on the same system, or separately. I made a mental note to check out how that worked as I stepped into the shower, not really aware that I was fully clothed.

Laughing at myself, I removed my clothes, even the shirt as far as it would go, hanging torn from the butcher knife. I removed that, too, with a scream at the top of my lungs—

I slipped and fell and crawled out of the bathroom, as if by putting distance from the site of my worst pain would lessen it somehow.

Rayna was still screaming on the bloody bed like a banshee. I didn't know why. I'd been the one knifed. I'd been the one doing all the knifing. I'd done all the work, after all.

I made it to my feet, reached back and found the closest towels and dried myself off, mixture of water and blood, and made my way to Izzy's closet. The producer was a little on the chubby size, but height-wise a good match, with the same shoe-size as well. I put on some nice duds, nothing fancy.

"Rayna, if you could stop screaming a minute, you need to get dressed and we need to get out of here before the police come and put us in the gas chamber, you understand?"

"I didn't do anything!" she screamed. "I just wanted to be in the movies!"

I laughed, which was probably the wrong thing to do right then.

"I'm calling the police," she stated, which calmed her hysterics considerably.

I froze, I have to admit. The phone was in her hand. She was my friend, my client, the one person in Hollywood I had come to love and trust. *By all rights, I should kill her,* I was thinking.

But I did not, do you believe that?

S-A-Y, remember. Stay Ahead of Yourself? Well, right then I needed to stay ahead of the law. I took a step in Rayna's direction—

She hit the button and my switchblade—the one I'd tossed on the bed a minute earlier—flipped out, pointed at me. I could see the power on her face, the goddamn "Girl Power" she felt at that moment, the MeToo deal.

"Fuck that," I said. "Go ahead and call the police."

I found one of Izzy's nicer jackets, warm and leather with fur lining, probably fake—

"Hello, 9-1-1?" Rayna was saying into her phone.

Of course it's 9-1-1—you dialed it, you big cow.

With a sarcastic wave, I was out of there. Down the stairs to the front door, stepping over the maid—she'd made it to the welcome mat, brave girl, before dying, good for her—and out the front door.

Outside it was cool but not cold. The jacket had been just right. I considered taking one of Izzy's cars, but decided no—why make it easy on them?

"Catch me if you can!" I barked softly into that good night. Not a great movie but I enjoyed it. DiCaprio is no Johnny Depp, but he's okay. I always wondered if he took movies like and *Wolf of Wall Street* just so he could legally do crazy shit.

CHAPTER 42

The phone rang in Rachel Landon's living room. She ran to it the same way she ran to it every time it rang, hoping against hope. Nine times out of ten it was someone trying to sell her something, or a charity, or a political call, or a "free offer" which Rachel Landon had no interest in because she knew a scam when she heard one. She tried not to be rude, but it was getting more and more difficult.

"Hello?" she answered.

"Hello," came a female voice at the other end. "Is this Rachel Landon?"

"Who is this?" Mrs. Landon asked a little testily.

"This is the Los Angeles Police Department, Operations, Pacific Division."

Rachel Landon gasped and sat down hard on the couch.

"This is Rachel Landon," she said, crying already. It wasn't George. If it was good news, it would be George himself.

"Mrs. Landon, do you own a Chrysler 300 vehicle?"

"My husband does. George Landon. Have you found him? Tell me quick. Is he dead? I need to know." She started crying—

"We've found the car," the woman said.

"My husband?"

"I don't know about that. Is he missing?"

"Yes, in Los Angeles. He's a private detective. He went there to look for someone and was never seen or heard from again."

"When was this?"

"It's been...six weeks now."

The phone seemed to go dead.

"Hello? Are you still there?" Mrs. Landon asked.

"Yes, I'm still here," the woman at the other end of the phone answered. "I am Officer LaTonya Lewis and I'm going to walk you through this. As long as it takes. We have not found your husband deceased. We have not found your husband alive, either."

"Thank you," Rachel sighed.

Maybe now...after all this time...maybe there'd be news about Larry, too...

CHAPTER 43

Detective Hoffsberger drove by the Arbuckle Apartment on Sunset. He hit the brakes. He knew the place. He knew it very well, too well. It couldn't hurt to ask. Hoffsberger found a place to park, legally—no reason to announce his presence.

He rang the bell and scouted the area—usual crowd: druggies, prostitutes (male/female ratio 2:1 this night), lost tourists, guys coming home from work, that work might be selling drugs, maybe something else—

"Yes?" came the voice on the intercom.

"I'd like to talk," Hoffsberger announced, showing his badge discretely to the camera above the door.

The manager buzzed him in. Hoffsberger got right down to business, wordlessly holding up the photograph of Jack C. Cunningham, actor.

The building manager snickered.

"What'd he do?" the man asked.

"You know him?" Hoffsberger asked.

"Yeah, he's up on four—"

"What room?"

"I don't know—what am I? Kreskin?"

"Go look it up. Now. STAT. ASAP. Got it?"

Hoffsberger could hear the panic in his own voice; the manager sensed it too. They both thought the other was about to wet his pants.

"Really doesn't look like him, though," the manager said as he found his legs and scrambled into the office. "Doesn't do him justice at all. He's a very handsome young man, you know."

"No, I didn't," Hoffsberger replied. "Which room?" the detective repeated.

"Four forty-seven," the manager replied, looking at his chart on the wall. "You want me to go up with you?"

"What for?"

"Because I have the key," the manager answered, grabbing the key from a cabinet on the wall, heading out of the office. The man had gone from deadly afraid to enthusiastic side-kick in less than a second—

"You don't need to see a search warrant?" Hoffsberger asked on their way down the hall.

"Nah, I know you."

"You do?"

"Yeah, you were here before. That Mavis Benning thing."

Hoffsberger remembered. The woman in the water-tank.

"You were here then?" Hoffsberger asked as they climbed up four floors.

"That's right. Biggest thing that ever happened to me, I'd say."

"Oh, sure," Hoffsberger said, leaving out the "man, *that's* sad" part.

"You, too, I imagine," the manager said. "It's how you became a detective, wasn't it?"

"Was it?" Hoffsberger stopped cold in the middle of the fourth floor hallway. He'd never quite understood exactly *how* he'd become a detective. "It was some sort of anti-gang operation—"

"No, you got it all wrong," the manager told the detective. "It was Mavis Benning—you found the body."

Hoffsberger knew *that* wasn't true. The manager had it all wrong. People remember funny things, sometimes the wrong things over time, and then somebody reappears and you put them in the old memory in the wrong place—

It's like that game Telephone—you whisper something around the room and when it gets to the last guy he jumps up and clobbers the first guy with a fungo bat—

Hoffsberger put up his hand to stop his own thoughts. He was afraid he was having a stroke. *What's the symptom? You smell toast, right? This whole fucking building smells like toast! And piss!*

The manager looked puzzled. "Elevator's down," he explained.

Hoffsberger tried to collect his thoughts. He needed to be alert. If there was a killer in the room there—the detective forgot the number already—Hoffsberger needed to be ready. A knife could be employed just as quickly as a gun—

The detective took out his service revolver and checked it was loaded and ready to go. He put it at his side and signaled silently for the manager to lead him on.

"Shouldn't you call for backup?" the manager asked.

Hoffsberger just shook his head. There's no way they'd send anybody, not unless he was shot and bleeding on the street somewhere, or already dead. There was too much explaining to do—Jack C. Cunningham who was really Porter Skully, with parents in Oregon, who maybe had killed the real Porter Skully just so he could take the poor slob's name—

Stop it, just stop it, Hoffsberger told himself. *You can't think yourself out of this. And help's not coming.*

Hoffsberger pressed his back against the wall and hung his pistol down at his side. He noted which way the door opened and positioned himself in exactly the right spot. Wordlessly, he instructed the manager to unlock the door and push it open, then jump back out of the way. They waited, Hoffsberger gathering his courage, life flashing before his eyes, mostly bad luck—

He signaled.

The manager turned the key, pushed the door open and jumped back. Hoffsberger charged in—

The TV was on. There was no other sound, no other person. The bathroom door was open, the shower curtain pulled to one side. There was no one there. No one to shoot. No one to shoot at Hoffsberger.

The detective deflated, a little disappointed after all that adrenalin.

The manager peeked in.

Hoffsberger jumped.

"Jesus! Don't sneak up like that!" he shouted. "I could've shot you!"

"He's not here?" the manager asked.

"No, he's not," the detective answered, annoyed. "Is there still a water-tower on the roof?"

The manager stared, thrilled and scared to death at the same time.

"It's still there," the man said. "I'll show you the way."

The first thing that struck Detective Hoffsberger when he climbed out onto the roof was just how beautiful it was. The moon was full, shining over the whole of lit-up Hollywood below, and the mountains above, full of movie stars, rich folk, and the real stars of the universe over it all. The Hollywood sign lit up the distance like an arc-light. Down Sunset Boulevard, or over on Hollywood Boulevard, a real klieg-light was lighting up the sky—some sort of movie premier.

It took Hoffsberger's breath away. Such as it was, this was his town.

The manager scrambled up onto the roof behind Hoffsberger, who whirled, managing not to kill the man for the second time in the last ten minutes.

Might as well pop him right now, the detective thought. *You know you're going to do it eventually.*

"Stay back," Detective Hoffsberger told the other man. Hoffsberger holstered his weapon, found a small flashlight in his coat pocket and climbed the six feet of ladder up to the water-tank. He figured out the catch to the quarter-lid—the lock was long gone. Legs a little wobbly on the ladder, the detective nevertheless managed to get the lid open and his head under the plate of metal.

He clicked the flashlight on.

It took a few seconds to register just exactly what he was looking at: human flesh and bones, half-decayed, time-warn, a mishmash of a coroner's nightmare.

Hoffsberger didn't know whether to laugh or cry.

"See anything?" the manager asked.

Naw, nothing, Hoffberger told himself. Aloud, he said, "Bingo..." flatly. He had no idea—was this good luck to find this...or was it bad luck?

CHAPTER 44

Somewhere in the world people go to parties to have fun, eat supper for the flavor and nourishment, take in a show for entertainment. In Hollywood, it's all to get ahead, to be seen, connect maybe, *belong*.

Me, Jack C. Cunningham—I ran for my life down the hills of Hollywood, looking for escape, a way out. I'd put all my eggs in one basket—Rayna Rourke—who turned out to be a basket-case at the end of it all, ha ha. "Put all my eggs in one basket-case," stupid me. Big joke.

They were gathered out front, about fifty people of various tribes—the usual: the free lunch types, the movie stars, sports stars, agents, celebrities, old and young, hangers-on, "friends-of," rich and super-rich and filthy rich—

What the hell?

I'd heard about these things, a night-time real estate open house as it turned out. A huge mansion, asking price $10 million or so. What better way to disappear?

I mingled among the hoi polloi. It would be a good place to hand out my photo and resume if I wasn't on the lam, actually, though it wouldn't have been cool, but then cool is overrated, especially if handing out my picture and resume got me an acting job.

Who do you have to fuck to get ahead in this town?

"Has Izzy gone in already?" I asked the lady who was giving out the "Keys to the Kingdom," which is what she called the gold keys (real gold, I'm guessing) that got you into the wing-ding.

"Izzy?"

"Izzy Clurman, the producer—"

"Not here," the woman at the door stated, suddenly turning cold as ice. I immediately realized she wasn't the real estate agent, just like the assistant real estate agent or something and she was determined at that moment not to let me inside. Maybe there was blood all over my jeans, shirt and jacket. I looked to be sure before I remembered I'd taken a shower and put on Izzy's clean clothes. I guess I was a little paranoid right then, or confused, what with everything that had happened—

"I was supposed to meet him here. I'm Izzy Clurman's assistant, see?"

"Well, he's not here."

"I should probably go on in and check it out," I told the woman, adding a smile for charm sake.

"Your invitation?"

"Izzy's got that, see?" I explained. "He might not even make it. I could get fired over something like this. He wanted to see this house. He's really anxious to move on account of all the extra money he has to invest in real estate."

The woman stared at me. She wasn't buying it, but then again, it wasn't really any skin off her nose. I think it was Izzy's designer clothes that convinced her, especially the fur-lined jacket.

"Okay," she said, "you can go in."

But she didn't step aside. She handed me a two-page document with tiny print, and a pen.

"What's this?" I asked.

"A liability waiver," she told me, like I was some kind of rube from the sticks and didn't know how they did things in the Big City, legal-wise that is.

"Oh, sure," I said convincingly. "Of course."

I skimmed the thing and signed it "Burford Hauser" or something, handed it back and scooted right inside, mission accomplished.

Other assistant realtor types handed out information packets on the property—$60 million was the asking price, apparently. I turned down the brochures—I figured I should keep my hands free.

The party was Biblically themed—Sodom and Gomorrah, to be specific. They had exotic animals—camels, leopards, a monkey cage—borrowed a ton from *Fellini Satyricon*, with some *Conan the Barbarian* thrown in. The party had a definite desert theme, and lots of Old Testament debauchery, harems, drinking, bestiality—that sort of thing. The house was on three floors and was otherwise "roadside hotel modern," its key feature separate swimming pools on all three levels, which poured down into each other, then pumped back to the highest one, apparently. You could hear the pump going a mile a minute, even over the blasting Middle Eastern music— sexy, exotic. The pools managed to be both inside and outside, with glass bottoms and walls. Dozens of topless mermaids swam around in two of them, and you could ogle their free-floating racks and scaly asses from every angle and through the glass. In the third pool, sharks and piranhas. A guard made sure nobody got too close.

I wandered the grounds acting like I was interested in buying the dump, grabbed a plate and a champagne flute and started chowing down on endangered species. The catering help all assured me it was genuine elephant and rhino and Bengal tiger. I'd say it tasted like chicken, but that'd just be a joke. It tasted like shit.

I started drinking like there was no tomorrow, which for the various species was true, I guess. All that killing had made me hungry, and the mermaids made me horny, but there wasn't much I could do about that, so I stuffed my face with California Condor—which *did* taste like chicken—and tried not to think about it.

"Do the piranhas and the sharks get along?" I asked the security man, making conversation. Everybody else looked like a phony baloney or an actor or actress, excuse the redundancy, or a realtor wanting to tell me all about the property. Who needs that?

"Pardon me, sir?" the guard asked over the music.

"I said, 'do the piranhas and sharks get along?'"

The man chuckled and shook his head. He told me in confidence:

"Sometimes the piranhas attack one of the sharks and then there's a lot of blood, which sends the sharks into frenzy and they start eating each other and the piranhas go nuts, too. Stick around, it could happen any minute."

"What do you do then?" I asked.

"I grab that pole over there—" He pointed. "—with the sharp, pointy thing at the end. I separate them as best as I can and generally not all of them die. Then again, what the hell do I care?"

A big, giant dominatrix with a hefty set of bazongas and a butt to die for, dressed in a really hot peek-a-boo leather outfit, roamed among the guests and gave them a spank on their butts if they wanted, lightly. *Amateurs.*

Lowanna Xanderson was there. I spotted her talking to some movie stars—I won't give their names—they can do their own goddamn publicity if they're that desperate. In fact, they were all looking at their Rolexes and Apple Watches or whatever was trendy in timekeeping at the moment, wondering when *Variety* and *Hollywood Reporter* would show up and take their pictures, the closest the two mags got to "news" anymore, having abandoned journalism to pursue glitzy Oscar ads and real estate ads (and BTW, expensive time-piece ads).

I wondered if I could maneuver Lowanna Xanderson over to the pool... one shove and she'd have to take her chances with the sharks and piranhas.

I laughed. It wouldn't work. They wouldn't touch her. "Professional courtesy." I love that joke.

The dominatrix was talking to a couple of other women. They seemed concerned, shaped eyebrows all scrunched down, glancing over to me a few times. One of them was the junior realtor at the door who'd let me in—probably lost her dorm-key or something. I tried to read their lips—why were they talking about me? Or was I just being paranoid? The word "Izzy" figured prominently in their vocabulary, it seemed to me, and they seemed angry.

I handed my champagne flute and plate of half-eaten, nearly extinct protein to the security man who'd become my best friend, told him "hold these for me, thank you," and headed into the house like I needed to check the plumbing and the heating and the air-conditioning and maybe the wi-fi and cable setup while I was at it, in a hurry, before making an offer on the dump.

The women followed in hot pursuit.

There was a fucking elevator but no stairs I could see. I ran like a crazy person, finally coming to an interior mezzanine walkway overlooking a living room on the floor below. The stairs were across the large opening, with a second dominatrix, even bigger than the first, charging up, ta-tas tapping a tango, whip in hand, screaming like a banshee: "There he is! There he is!"

The mob of women behind me didn't need the direction—they'd spotted me just fine on their own. I put one hand on the railing and swung over to the room below, aiming for the couch, bristling with confidence from a week of "Jim Delanie's Stunt-School Intensive."

The drop was further than I expected—twenty feet—twice what we'd tried in Delanie's class, liability exposure being what it is, and that was without having knifed a quartet of strong, vibrant people to death earlier in the evening, running all over the canyons and (oh yeah) a butcher knife stuck deep into my shoulder. So gimme a break and forgive me if I didn't stick the landing, instead bouncing off the edge of the couch, falling to the floor, hitting my head on the sharp corner of the coffee table. When I came to a nano-second later, the women were clattering down the stairs in their high heels, the second dominatrix in the lead, the first one trailing, a chorus of knockin' knobbies (my favorite Bobby Day song, incidentally) blasting my brain.

I shot up off the floor and made a run for it, right out into a crowd of "beautiful people," many of whom were household names, celebrities, movie and TV and recording artists, who I would have liked to have schmoozed with, and told them I was an actor, too, except there was an army of women screaming like Sergeant Rock and Easy Company:

"That's Izzy Clurman's assistant! Get the bastard!"

Suddenly I found myself face to face with Lowanna Xanderson, yelling "excuse me!" at the top of my lungs, going right (she went right), going left (she went left), screaming "get the fuck out of my way, bitch!" as I shot past her or thought I had, but she'd stuck out one of those gams of hers—she's so old she's got "gams" for crying out loud—and tripped me good. I went skittering, falling, flying into the pool with a theatrical splash—a cannonball prize-winner.

It wasn't the piranhas, it wasn't the sharks—worse. Mermaids—on me like Ariel's Legions from Hell, clawing at and scratching at my face and screaming at me because they thought I was associated with Izzy Clurman and his disgustingness, maybe 'cause I'd mentioned him at the door... With their legs wrapped together in their mermaid suits, there wasn't much kicking they could do, but their fists and fingernails were bad enough. Worse, the women who had chased me now surrounded the pool, egging the mermaids on.

"Kill him! Kill him!" they screamed, and the mermaids—six of them, I think—were doing their best to accommodate.

That's when that pole showed up somehow, the one with the sharp, pointy thing at the end, intended to separate sharks from each other, and from the piranhas. Now it was being wielded by Dominatrix #1, who wasn't trying to separate anything except maybe me from my head, me from my dick, me from my blood. With a long professional career, trained in delivering pain, the old bag had the skills and the moves, I had to admit. If I protected my crotch, she went for my neck. If I knocked the gaff from my neck, she poked at my balls. Meanwhile the blood was flowing—my blood—and the mermaids had given up on gouging my eyes out, opting instead for holding me under and trying to drown me.

Somehow above all the screaming and mayhem and chlorinated suffocation I heard the distant sound of a police siren. The girls heard it, too, and maybe they decided homicide wasn't a good look for their mermaid career pictures and resumes. However it happened, I got away, crawled out of the pool, dodged a camel, a lowland gorilla, two recording executives and a black-faced mime, and hightailed it around the back of the house before getting killed or critically maimed.

I jumped the fence, OJ style, and made it out to another one of those craggy, tree-lined alleys—steep, overlit and overparked. I half ran, half fell downhill, careening my way in the shadows as a police helicopter suddenly appeared above, soaring over me like a dragon in *Game of Thrones*. The "midnight sun" of its giant light came on, lighting up the whole canyon but somehow missing me, hidden behind a Maserati, the cheaper one, the coupe.

There'd be news copters soon, to join the cop copters, looking. For me.

I started walking, slowly now. If I kept cool and walked slowly, they wouldn't spot me maybe, even though no one ever walked in this neighborhood. Even the Mansons had driven up there.

I slipped into the next canyon through a couple of multi-million dollar properties, abandoned, for sale. Dogs barked, sirens screamed out and the cop copter stayed waaaay too long, but the media never showed up—

Car chase, I figured.

Eventually I found myself walking around West Hollywood feeling like a stranger in a strange land. It was almost midnight—would I turn into something else then? People stared, sensing I was dangerous, a human like them but *not* like them, alien and deadly, like in *The Thing,* or *Invasion of the Body Snatchers.* The hell of it was: they were *right.* But how did they know?

I looked down at myself. Maybe I was bleeding. Maybe I'd wet myself or left my dick hanging out like a forgetful grandfather after a couple of drinks at Christmas.

Nothing. No reason whatsoever. They sensed it, I could tell, but how? That I was unfit to live amongst them. I reached for my knife. I couldn't kill them all...or could I? No, I couldn't. I'd left my knife in Rayna's hands at Izzy's place. If I ever got out of this alive, I vowed to get *two* knives, one for my pocket, the second for backup in my sock or something. Maybe *three* knives. And a gun.

People come to LA for a lot of reasons, to act, to write, to make movies, to make music. Many of them just come to die. Eucalyptus trees included. Non-native species, not exactly suited for the sandy soil. Fall over like the town slut in the faintest wind, burned like your deepest desire in the frequent fires.

Don't be naive. Movies are meant to influence and manipulate us. Why do some movies get made and others don't? Why do some movies get shown and others don't? They're reviewed, maybe play a couple of film festivals, then they're buried, in favor of the latest comic book. Why? Who's behind that? They'll be quick to tell you it's the marketplace, "demographics," luck of the draw, the same way they'll tell you the stock market's honest and the world's not going straight to a fiery hell, oceans first, sky next, earth last.

I found myself on Holloway Drive, a little cut-off, slash of a street between Santa Monica Boulevard and Sunset in West Hollywood, famous for nothing except it's where Sal Mineo got knifed to death in the winter of 1976, in the alley next to his cheap-shit apartment. Before my time, though the knife was skillfully employed, the way I like to do it, but to the chest—I like the throat. No, the reason the case connected with me: him being a handsome young actor at one time like me, tragically killed in the prime. Apparently liked to party (same here) and except for the gay part of it (him, not me), like I had a twin. Cursed, like everybody on *Rebel Without a Cause*: James Dean dead in 1955, Natalie Wood to come in '81, another unsolved murder. The dude led two lives, at least, and kept them separate but equal until the last mistake, obviously, that did him in. He partied with so many guys and did so many drugs, only a genius could keep it straight (no pun intended). He knew how to put it all under wraps, obviously. Like I said, *role model.*

Only I understand the dude, I'll guarantee you that. The lonely nights. Trying to fill them with the next sex partner, the next sex act—"what's your name again?" You can get lost in this city, I tell you, even when you know exactly who you are and where you're going. Watch his movies sometimes. It's all in his eyes. He'd be old enough to be my Dad at this point. Grandfather even. I don't know—you do the math. Did he get off easy, getting knifed in the prime of life, dying a legend? Did the dude who did it do him a huge, fucking favor?

Hell, I don't know. Maybe I'm just a guy on a mission, ending people's existence before they suffer the slings and arrows, getting old, heart disease, erectile dysfunction, hemorrhoids, pulmonary artery disease and the old folks home.

To those I helped by ending their misery early...you're welcome.

CHAPTER 45

Detective Hoffsberger waited all alone in a room across the hall from Jack C. Cunningham's place, aka Porter Skully, in the Arbuckle Apartments. Hoffsberger's call for more detectives had been denied repeatedly.

"There's been a murder at Izzy Clurman's place," came the reply.

"Who's that?"

"Big producer, apparently," the dispatcher told Hoffsberger, "how do I know? What am I—Hedda Hopper?"

"Who?" Hoffsberger asked again, completely confused.

"We got a multiple murder in the hills," the dispatcher explained slowly, patiently, as to a child. "A four-banger. Knives. Lots of blood. Show-biz. The media's all over it—not helping! Same time some commotion at a big party not far away. With sharks, mermaids and some sort of harpoon-wielding strap-on jockey."

"Huh...?"

"Just handle it yourself," the dispatcher advised. "We're full-up here."

"I got a serial killer, I got cannibalism, I got dead bodies rotting in a water-tank—"

"Just another night in Tinsel Town, dude. Just another night in Tinsel Town..."

The man hung up.

Detective Hoffsberger sat stunned. He wondered if he shouldn't call the media himself. Get some stooge from Channel 7 News up there—"Exclusive. Breaking News. Only on 7. Cannibal arrested. More at eleven. And weather."

<hr />

They arrested Rayna on suspicion of murder and took her right to Cedars-Sinai for a medical evaluation and psychiatric checkup. To say she was in shock would have been an understatement. Worried for her health, the detectives gave her one phone call, on her own phone, in the back of the police car:

"I'm coming home, Mom and Dad. I'm coming home."

Back in Nekoosa, Wisconsin, north of Petenwell Lake, Millie and Marston Baker went crazy with excitement and relief. They laughed, jumped up and down and cried, then tried calling their daughter Julie back. By then, the police had confiscated her phone.

<hr />

There was no way I'd make it back to the Arbuckle. My shoulder hurt like crazy. Scale of 1 to 10, it was an 11, like that amp in *This is Spinal Tap*. I'd lost a great deal of blood. My head spun like tomorrow's headline news. I should have gone to a hospital but that would have been insane. They'd have me locked up in a minute, they'd have my DNA, they'd connect me to the mess in the canyon, with Izzy Clurman, maybe even the other Porter Skully, the two-bit hack actor.

The Brite Lite Motel off of Sunset offered itself to me, an oasis in the desert. I walked into the office.

"What happened to you?" the clerk wanted to know.

I guess I looked pretty bad—

"Mudslide," I told him.

"Mudslide? It hasn't rained in a month."

"*Delayed* mudslide. The rain undermined the land under the pool in the house above me and it all came right down on my head."

Hurt as I was, I could still spin a yarn—

"Man, you want me to call an ambulance?"

"No, no ambulance. Just give me a room."

"Big boy, huh?" the clerk said. "Handle yourself, can you?"

I didn't need the man's snark, but there wasn't anything I could do about it. I was in too much pain and my trusty blade was back at Izzy's in Rayna's tight fist.

"Just gimme a room," I repeated.

"We only got one," he said.

"That's all I need."

"What you *need* is medical attention, bro."

"Give me the room."

"I should warn you about it," the clerk said.

"What?"

"Marilyn Monroe fucked a city councilman to death in that room—"

I laughed. I couldn't stop laughing. Was that a drawback somehow? Or was he going to charge extra for that?

"You're turning me on," I managed to say through the tears of laughter. The joke was killing me—

"He comes back sometimes," the clerk told me, dead serious. "The councilman. She does, too—"

I slapped a couple hundred-dollar bills on the counter.

"Key."

"Okay, but you were warned," the clerk said, handing me the key—not some slide-card thing but the real deal, 50s, diamond-shaped.

It was a big mistake. I should have listened. All night long the ghost of the councilman haunted the room, along with Marilyn Monroe. She was naked and gorgeous; he was naked and not. They were making a porn film, which they called a "stag" film and it was all in black and white and since I was in the fucking bed trying to get some sleep and not bleed to death they went ahead and fucked all over me. All the while a bunch of cigar-smoking guys in old-fashioned undershirts, nothing on underneath, fat hard-ons poking out from under their fat bellies, laughed and poked and egged the participants on, while the director, Freddy Weaver, was showing them how to fuck "the correct way" using some idiot method he'd learned at Konstantin fucking Stanislavsi's knee. Clyde what's-his-name from acting class was there, too, yelling at everybody to "get back to Jesus" until somebody kicked him out and they kept on filming with huge arc-lights in the tiny room, and a giant camera the size of a refrigerator—Technicolor 3-stripe, I'm pretty sure—except they didn't bother loading any film all in it. It was all "linguine loads," apparently, which I understood to mean there was no film, just the fun of fucking each other and watching them fuck each other, scamming the actors who believed it was on film and they'd be stars—

In the end, Marilyn got fed up and angry, which was very attractive, and shot the councilman in the nuts first, then the chest, then she bit off my dick and ate it while I was screaming "Why me?! What did I do?!" and that's when I woke up feeling like I hadn't slept at all.

CHAPTER 46

LA Police Detective Michael M. Hoffsberger staked out the room across from Porter Skully aka Jack C. Cunningham for a full 72 hours before the story was leaked to the press and the stakeout was blown. During the three days, the subject never returned to his room. Once the media got hold of the story, they virtually abandoned the Izzy Clurman quadruple murder as well as the "Party from Hell" incident nearby that same night. This latest scene had the history of the Arbuckle going for it as well as the bones in the water-tank, plus the cannibalism. In all, the remains of seven people were found, though not all positively identified.

Detective Hoffsberger was ambushed by the press on a number of occasions, and became so well-known for his terse and angry "no-comments" that he was soon parodied on late-night talk-shows.

On a hunch, Hoffsberger compared DNA found at the Arbuckle to the Skullys in Oregon and found a familial connection. It turned out not to be necessary, however, since Porter Skully aka Jack C. Cunningham had recently submitted his DNA to one of those online heredity websites. A perfect match.

When Hoffsberger learned that detectives in the Izzy Clurman murder investigation had obtained DNA which did not fit any of the know participants—Izzy, the two women, the maid, or Rayna Rourke—Hoffsberger, on another hunch, suggested they compare their mystery sample with Hoffsberger's findings at the Arbuckle. Once again, the detective was right.

Once Porter Skully aka Jack C. Cunningham had been identified in the press, the two parents were besieged by the media who surrounded their Oregon farm.

"We don't know where Porter is," they explained, "and we don't believe all the things they're saying about him."

"That cannibalism thing is total baloney," Mack Skully proclaimed. "He would never do that."

"He even flirted with vegetarianism," Rose Skully added in a high, meek voice. "Not for long, and not totally—I mean he wasn't a nut about it. But dietetically that's as far out as our Porter got, I'm sure."

Me? I was ready to throw up.

America fell in love with the elderly Skullys just as the world grew to hate me with every new outrage that hit the news. My so-called parents showed the press the well-kept farm/ranch grounds and the comfortable quarters. They described how they'd taken down the fences and had no problem sharing their crops with the local deer and other wildlife in the neighborhood.

"We're organic, cruelty free, free-range all the way," Mack lied ridiculously.

They debunked the notion that the property was a "compound" of some kind, or a religious sect—

"We're Unitarians, for cryin' out loud," Rose Skully chuckled deeply, a hint of gravel in her voice, a cold coming on. Her smile was endearing, and Mack had patted her arm as if to say, "our religious beliefs—Unitarian or otherwise—are nobody's business."

Did I mention I thought I was going to throw up?

"This is where Porter put on his little plays," Mack showed the youngest member of the *60 Minutes* news operation. It was a small but sturdy open-air stage about fifty yards from the house, built of wood, oiled and polished. "It's a fairly accurate one-quarter scale model of the Globe Theatre," Mack stated proudly. "That's where Shakespeare put on his plays, you know."

Rose gently elbowed Mack—Unitarians or not, there was no reason to brag.

I did throw up.

"We encouraged Porter, we really did," Rose stated, waving her hand palms-up at the stage, offering it up as evidence. "All that business about us beating him or starving him or all that—that's total nonsense."

"Total," Mack agreed.

Alone in my motel room, in the middle of "fly-over hell," half-way to New York, all I could do was steam. My so-called parents, the bastards, were making their case and garnering all the fame, whereas me, Jack C. Cunningham, as a wanted fugitive of the law, could only sit and watch.

They splashed my 8 x 10 glossy all over the screen but that didn't matter to me—everybody knows an actor's picture doesn't look anything like them and nobody was going to spot me based on that.

After that night of Hell at the Brite Lite Motel, I tried going back to the Arbuckle but at the last minute I got spooked—maybe it was one of the ghosts there—all I know is a voice told me to take it on the lam and scram but quick, like an over-cranked scene in a Keystone Kops 1-reeler.

I had some money and bought some new clothes that didn't smell like chlorine, blood, mermaids and Izzy Clurman. I took the Sunset bus east from Hollywood through Little Armenia, Thai Town, Silverlake, and Echo Park until Sunset Boulevard turned into Cesar Chavez downtown, ending up at Union Station.

From there it was bus, Amtrak and hitchhiking to New York City, just the way the old-timers did back in the day before air-travel ruined everything.

CHAPTER 47

Rayna Rourke, in countless interviews with the authorities, told them all about Jack. Nobody believed her except Hoffsberger, who came to visit daily at the psychiatric wing of the county lockup. In the end, they figured Rayna was lying and so was Hoffsberger, because the detective had become obsessed with Rayna and Jack Cunningham. They concluded anything Hoffsberger had to say was a lie to protect her. Ignoring the press coverage concerning "Jack/Porter, Actor/Killer," believing it all a ruse like OJ's "real killer," the District Attorney eventually charged Rayna with the four murders at Izzy Clurman's house. Life in prison without the possibility of parole was what they asked for. The death penalty had been iffy for decades in California, and there was tremendous sympathy for any woman who got entangled with the notorious Izzy Clurman.

When Rayna's lawyer suggested she plead guilty and beg for mercy—

"The victims' blood was all over you, Rayna; the murder weapon was in your hand when the police arrived—"

—Rayna hired a new attorney based on privately given advice from Lowanna Xanderson.

A day later, famed palimony/divorce/sexual harassment lawyer Brenda Bluestone was allowed into Rayna's locked room in the secure facility.

Rayna told the internationally recognized figure that it was all a misunderstanding, and that Jack Cunningham had killed those people at Izzy Clurman's house while defending her—Rayna—from great bodily harm, and that he would soon turn himself in, sacrificing himself, and would explain the whole thing and set her—Rayna—free because he loved her—Rayna—and wouldn't want her to go to prison for something he—Jack—did himself.

Brenda Bluestone waited patiently while Rayna told her story, only checking email once and glancing at her watch two times. She took no notes.

"Thank you for telling me that, Julie," Brenda Bluestone told Rayna when Rayna finally stopped talking. "Have you told that to anyone else?"

"Yes, everybody. Especially Detective Hoffsberger. He's very nice."

"Well, that may be, Rayna, but I don't think you should talk to him anymore, or anyone else for that matter. Only me."

"Why?" Rayna asked. "This is all a mistake—"

"Just hear me out, if you will," the lawyer said. "Right now you're very famous as 'the woman who brought Izzy Clurman down.' You're a hero, and if anybody doubts that, I can get a hundred women to testify to what Mr. Clurman did to them. So, here's the choice—you can say some low-life guy named Jack did it, which is gonna be tough to prove, and people are gonna believe you or maybe not. Maybe a jury might even buy it, or not, and let you off with manslaughter, which gets you out in five years after some very hard time—"

Rayna swallowed hard. Brenda Bluestone knew she had her hooked.

"Or..." the attorney said, "you can say you killed Izzy Clurman in self-defense after he did horrible things to those women and was going to do the same to you. I can help supply details if you need them. True facts, true details, just maybe they didn't happen to you specifically, understand? You're a hero, and no jury is going to convict you or blame you for anything, but more important is the fact the world will know your name and want to see more of you. Certainly I can land a book deal, perhaps a movie-of-the-week, or a plain old movie. Everybody wants you on their talk show. Everybody wants to put you in their movie."

Rayna gasped—her dream coming true—

"Am I making sense here?" the attorney asked.

Rayna nodded vigorously—

"My old friend Lowanna Xanderson called again this morning—"

"She did?" Rayna almost screamed—

"She's a dear, dear friend. She's the one who recommended I represent you, you know."

"I know—"

"And maybe we'll use her, maybe we won't," Bluestone said. "The fact is you're bigger even than Lowanna Xanderson now, Julie—"

"Call me Rayna—"

"I like Julie better. It conveys a certain innocence. From now on I think you should be Julie Baker again."

"There are a lot of actresses named Julie Baker," Rayna protested.

"Oh, that doesn't matter."

"It doesn't—?"

"No, not at all."

"Okay. 'Julie.' That's okay with me," Rayna agreed.

"So we're agreed on the rest of it, too?"

"I'll tell them I killed Izzy Clurman after he did things to those women," Rayna said. "Did he stab them, too?" Rayna asked, a little confused.

"Yes, I think he did," Bluestone answered. "And the maid."

"Yes, after he killed the maid, he stabbed the other two women," Rayna confirmed.

"You're very sorry it had to happen that way but you didn't have a choice," Bluestone coached, "because after he killed those women you knew he was going to kill you."

"Exactly."

"Good."

They smiled, both of them.

CHAPTER 48

Five years later.

Detective Hoffsberger checked every single day. There was no sign of Jack C. Cunningham aka Porter Skully anywhere in the world. He seemed to have disappeared into thin air. Hoffsberger hoped he was dead. His own life had fallen into a dreary routine. A few more years and he could retire. His daughter was working in movies, not as an actress, but in set decoration.

George Landon's wife and Larry Gregg's wife still waited for word on their husbands, whose bodies were never found. Neither was identified in bones from the Arbuckle Hotel. Once or twice a year, the two widows corresponded via email, and commiserated. Neither remarried.

Julie Baker became a big star. Everybody knew she would. She had real talent. Everybody could see that. She did a few small, independent projects first, just to get her feet wet and a couple of Oscar campaigns under her belt (no wins yet) before graduating to one or two huge blockbusters a year, mostly based on comic books. She appeared on a number of talk-shows promoting her various projects, but the hosts and public insisted she always speak about "that night" at Izzy Clurman's house in the canyons. There was a rumor she and OJ Simpson had a "Talent Discovery Show" in the works.

Me? I'm doing okay now. I'm auditioning for things here in New York—mostly off-Broadway but also some indie films. Taking music lessons, voice lessons, a little dance, too. I'll be okay.

I have a new name. I won't tell you what it is.

Later.

THE END